OMEGA FOR PROTECTIVE ALPHA

Wolf Shifter MPREG Fated Mates Romance

Michael Levi

1st edition

ISBN: 9798406207963
Imprint: Independently published

Cover design by: Michael Levi

CONTENTS

CHAPTER 1

My heart was pounding harder than it had ever been. I was in a big room with my father, who was determined to show me that he'd found me my fated mate.

I couldn't believe that, after all this time, he still thought that way about it. I mean, when was the last time we had a marriage where someone was supposed to marry a certain someone else?

I was pacing back and forth in the room, my hand on my chin as I thought about all the possibilities. I wanted to consider all the possibilities which involved me getting out of this unharmed. I sighed, realizing that I was in trouble deeper than I thought.

I stopped in front of a ball by one of the sides of the room. I looked around me as I took in the fact that it was in a special place.

It was like a small house in the room and it was big enough just to house the sphere. I almost put my hand on it, but I didn't do it. I knew that it would have been wrong and that my father wouldn't have liked it.

I jumped when I felt something setting on my shoulder. I snapped my head around, looking over it. It was my father who was behind me and he was looking at the sphere on the pillar in the house, happiness and comfort in his eyes.

It was like he was telling me he was accomplishing something he had been dreaming about for a very long time.

"When you both put your hands on it, hopefully it'll tell me that you were indeed made for each other, just like the foreseer told me. He's never been wrong in his life."

My father was an Alpha and even though he had a strong scent, I couldn't feel it. Not the way I could feel other Alphas' scents, though.

He was tall and imposing, and I could tell why my other father married him. They were matched together just like it was happening to me now. They went to the foreseer and he told them that they were fated mates.

Back in his time, that was normal and expected of them, but nowadays I loved someone else and I sure as hell wasn't going to marry a biker.

He also came from a very powerful and influential family in the city, but he was different. He was rough, aggressive, and always thought so highly of himself. He was the opposite of me.

How could my father even think that we were going to be a good match?

"When I put my hand there and it tells me that I'm supposed to marry Ish instead, then what? Will you lock me up until you can change what the sphere says?" I asked, realizing I might be making a mistake. After all, my dad was just looking out for what was best for me.

He narrowed his eyes slightly, taking his hand off my shoulder. "Cogwyn should be here any second now." He stepped away from me and went to the door out of the room.

It was a room in a church, and from here we could see the street outside. I couldn't see any cars or motorcycles driving on the road or pedestrians on the sidewalks. We were alone here, almost like the world was trying to tell me that it had moved on from this kind of custom.

I went to the door with my father and I stopped in my tracks when I heard the rumbling of a motorcycle as it pulled over.

It was Cogwyn, riding his motorcycle without a helmet on. He put his right foot on the ground, swung his leg over the motorcycle, and then turned so that he was looking at me.

I spoke with him maybe once in my life and I wasn't looking forward to this. He was the kind of guy who just didn't make sense to me. He was rich and could become a CEO, and yet he was doing this. He decided to become a biker to get one up on his father, who was very similar to my dad. He also believed in fated mates.

I shook my head, whirled around, and then went to where the small house was in the church. I had no idea why it even was in the church of all places it could be. All I knew was that it was making me hate this whole thing more than I already did.

"What do you think you're doing?" My father asked, making a beeline to me.

"Getting this over with as soon as possible. This thing here is probably broken anyway. Regardless of what it tells me, I'm not going to marry that asshole."

My father put both of his hands on my shoulders, staring into my eyes. He was making me feel uncomfortable and he knew that.

"You are going to follow our tradition and carry it on. Don't disappoint me on this, Bren. Your Omega father probably thinks the same way."

I opened my mouth to rebuke him, only to realize that a certain scent was impregnating the room in the church. I was in front of the small house where the sphere was when I realized it was the Alpha's scent I was feeling. It was strong, thick, and it was like it was making it very hard for me to breathe.

I went to the side just to see him stepping into the church, a devilish smile on his face. As an Omega who had turned 18 not too long ago, I was horny most of the time, and I couldn't even control it. I couldn't even try to control it because it was just something that my body did.

I closed my nose with my hand, earning a scoff from Cogwyn.

He just walked past me and then went to the sphere, looking down with disdain at it.

"So, you're telling me that this thing will prove I'm supposed to marry this piglet?" He asked, disdain in his voice.

My father wasn't one to let anyone impose themselves and make fun of me and of his traditions, so he strode toward the biker and put himself right in front of him, staring at his eyes as he showed how determined he was about doing this.

"Any reason why your father didn't come here as well? He should have come here with you by now."

Cogwyn stared back at my father, not saying or doing anything. It was like sparkles of electricity were flying between their eyes. I knew that my father didn't look at Cogwyn with good eyes, but he still believed in the tradition more than any other person in the city did.

I guess I got lucky and unlucky at the same time. Things could certainly be worse right now if I was part of another family.

"He should be coming here soon," Cogwyn growled, stepping away from my father and then to the sphere in the small house.

He was lifting his hand when my father warned, "You can't touch it until your father is also here with us. You need to follow traditions like everyone else."

"Like everyone else? Nobody even does this anymore…" I heard him mumbling to himself, showing me that he was tough and brave, but not against my father. In a fair fight, I knew that he would beat him easily. He would wipe the floor with him.

I stepped toward them and was lifting my hand to get their attention when I realized a limousine was pulling over. I snapped my head toward it, realizing that it was Cogwyn's dad who was coming.

One of the guards opened the door of the limousine for him and he stepped out of it, adjusting his tie. Guards surrounded him as he walked into the church. He stopped by my father, who shook his hand.

"Parth, it's so good to see you again, my friend. I've been waiting for this moment since the foreseer told us about it."

"Same here. And first things first, we need to follow the first step. This won't happen the way we want unless we do it."

Misk chuckled, putting a hand on my father's shoulder as they went to the small house. They stopped in front of the sphere on the pillar and started to mumble about something. I was a bit lost about what was happening, being someone who didn't care about these traditions at all.

I turned my head left, realizing that Cogwyn wasn't even paying attention to what our fathers were doing. He was leaning against one of the walls, arms crossed over his chest.

It was now, just like so many other times I was with him, that I couldn't help but notice the tattoos on his arms. They almost covered the entirety of them and that, coupled with his short hair, determined eyes, and a beard to be made, made him look like a thug.

I shivered, thinking that our parents were planning on making us live together for the rest of our lives.

CHAPTER 2

Cogwyn

Why I was wasting time with this was beyond me. I supposed it was because I respected my father way too much and he didn't respect what I wanted. I uncrossed my arms from my chest when it looked like this was finally ending.

"So, can I finally put my hands on the sphere?" I asked, pretending that my 'fated' Omega wasn't by my side. He had a scent, but it wasn't strong and I could ignore it easily. That's what I was doing. Bren tsked, crossing his arms over his chest as he looked away.

Good, I thought. I liked him better when he showed me he didn't like me at all.

Parth turned his eyes to look at me and I felt conflicted feelings coming from him. It was obvious that he didn't like me as a person. After all, I was a biker and a member of the 1%. I was never going to be a good guy.

Nevertheless, he believed in the traditions and in what the foreseer told him that day.

"Yes, now it's time," he answered as he stepped away with my father. I studied his face as I hoped he was going to change his mind and tell me that we didn't have to do this.

But that wasn't going to happen and the Omega was already

standing by my side, in front of the sphere. It was glowing like it was calling for us.

I tsked, saying, "I just get this over with before I break it."

Bren didn't look at me, putting his right hand on the sphere as I put my left hand on it. It was warm, which was weird. I had no idea if the sphere was supposed to be this hot.

It glowed brighter all of a sudden, the light drawing me to it and making me feel like I was in a dream. Moments later, it dimmed and returned to its normal state. The temperature of the sphere dropped and I knew that soon it was going to say what it thought of us.

I moved my hand away from the sphere, stepping away from it. It wasn't that it scared me, but that I already knew I wasn't going to like the answer it had for us. Our parents stepped closer to the sphere, their eyes glowing in expectation.

This was incredibly important to them.

"Bren and Cogwyn-" the sphere was saying when a shot echoed in the room, hitting Bren's father right in his eye. I saw the hole that it made there, his body falling limp on the floor. Bren screamed and I felt sorry for him for the first time in my life.

A round of shots came from one of the windows, catching my father off-guard. He was running toward me when he fell over the floor, his body not moving anymore. Pain wrenched my heart as I realized I didn't know what I should be doing.

Bikers from the Bear Bikers' gang were storming the church, pointing their weapons at us. Bren yelled for his father to wake up as he rushed over to him, but a shot to the ground, right in front of his right foot, stopped him in his tracks.

My hand shot to my gun and I pulled it out. I aimed it and shot at the first guy I could see, a Bear Biker with a smug on his face.

He fell to the floor as his hand grabbed at his chest. His hand looked for his submachine gun, but I was already shooting at him in his head before he could do anything.

I grabbed Bren's hand and tugged at it when I realized that he was holding his ground. Snapping my head to him, I barked, "Do you want to die here with everyone or come with me? They're attacking us and they won't stop coming."

"I'm not leaving my father behind!" He argued, making me feel a little sorry for him. A tear was rolling down his cheek and I knew that he wanted to make sure his father was okay, but it was too late for that.

He should be thankful that he didn't die slowly. He got shot to his eye. I didn't think he even realized what was happening.

I aimed my pistol and shot at another biker in his head, his body falling through the window and then plopping on the floor. I yanked the little Omega to me with all of my strength, hurting him. I pulled him up so that he was looking straight into my eyes.

"I don't think I need to explain the situation to you, or do I?" I growled, my canines growing bigger as my nose felt all kinds of strong scents around us. Most of them were Alphas.

If they turned now, I wouldn't be able to fight against them. We wouldn't come out of this alive and this little Omega knew that very well.

He was cute, with round and rosy cheeks, but I didn't have time to sweeten my words. I had to shoot another biker that was storming into the church and hid behind the pillar, the Sphere of Revelations exploding into a million pieces right above our heads.

Bren screamed and I covered his mouth with my hand. I looked into his eyes as he studied my face. "Look, we're getting out of here and I'm going to take you home. I promise you that."

"But-"

"No buts. We need to get out of here before more of them come and this escalates. We don't have a lot of time." I felt the smoothness and the softness of his hand, wondering what it would be like if-

I shook my head, deciding not to think about that right now. It wouldn't do me any good.

I popped over the pillar, shot at a handful more of bikers, and

then studied the room in the church. Spotting an exit, I jumped with the Omega and then leaped through the window, rolling outside with him. I was still gripping his hand tightly, and I wasn't going to let go of it.

The truth was that I cared about him, even if only at this moment. I knew what those Bear Bikers were looking for or, rather, who.

If and when they had their grubby hands on this Omega, they would do unspeakable things to him. I was part of the 1% just like them, but there were still things I'd never do.

"Let's go!" I shouted, tugging Bren with me as we sped over to Desire. My motorcycle was parked in an alleyway, hidden from everyone's eyes.

We heard speeding footsteps behind us, and I popped two shots at them. I missed as they ducked behind cover.

I tsked, getting to my bike, turning it on as I realized that Bren wasn't sitting on it. His eyes kept going up and down like he couldn't believe what was happening.

Meanwhile, I couldn't believe that he was hesitating right at the moment when I needed him to come with me.

"Look, I don't like having to save you any more than you do, but those guys killed your bodyguards and our fathers. We don't have another choice. We need to go to your house and, when we get there, you won't have to ever see me again, I promise."

I was actually looking forward to that.

He nodded, swinging his leg over the motorcycle as he wrapped his arms around my torso. I felt warmth in my heart as he did that, almost like I was enjoying it. But I shouldn't be feeling that way about it, I thought.

I twisted the handlebars of the motorcycle, stepped on it, and then rode away as fast as I could to where his house was. He lived in a mansion far from where we were. It was going to take me a lot of time to get there.

I heard bullets whizzing past our ears as I kept on speeding up

Desire. I pulled out my pistol, turned around without taking my hand off the left handlebar of the motorcycle, and then popped some shots in the heads of the bikers that were chasing us.

Bren ducked and buried his head on my back, tightening his arms around me. I wasn't going to deny that I felt a little sorry for him and better about him than I ever did in my life.

I studied the roads behind us as I realized that the bikers weren't chasing us anymore. I eased my grip on the handlebars of the motorcycle, turned to the left, and then cruised toward his house.

I had no idea how his Omega father was going to take it, but I was sure he was going to be better there.

CHAPTER 3

Bren

The fact that he was taking me to my house instead of abandoning me was a lot more than I expected from him. I was still with my arms wrapped around his torso and I wasn't thinking about pulling myself away from him anytime soon. The fact was that I needed someone to make me feel safe, even if it was the person I most hated in my life.

My father just died and he died thinking I hated him. I hated myself because I didn't tell him how important he was to me.

I should have told him that I was okay with his traditions and that we could work something out. Maybe I could have convinced him about marrying me to Ish instead.

But it was too late now for that, I thought as a tear rolled down my cheek. I pulled my head back as I studied the environment around me.

We were already leaving downtown and I couldn't even see cars or other bikes near us. It was almost like we were alone here or that someone was watching us.

"You can take your arms off my body now," Cogwyn growled, his earring blinking under the moonlight. It wasn't a full moon and I knew that he wasn't going to turn, thank goodness. I wouldn't know what to do if he did.

"But I'll fall off the bike if I do that."

He twisted the handlebars of the motorcycle as he sped through a red light. I widened my eyes, looking flabbergasted that he did that.

"No, you won't, and I don't like it when people like you get attached to me."

"You just rode through a red light. That's an infraction."

Cogwyn blinked twice, almost like he couldn't believe that I just said that. Then, he started to laugh as he turned his attention back to the road.

"Of course I did that. Did you think I was going to follow all the rules of how to drive properly when we're running for our lives?"

He peeked over his shoulder, his smirk taunting me and making me hate him more than I already did. Seeing that, I pushed myself away from him and gripped the sides of his motorcycle.

Fine. If he was going to keep being the asshole he'd always been, then I wanted as much distance from him as possible, even if that meant possibly hurting myself.

I was gripping the sides of his motorcycle as tightly as I could, so I was hoping it wasn't going to come to that. He did slow down his motorcycle, still cruising in the streets. I saw buildings and the houses moving past us, the golden and glowing light bulbs making the city look less gritty in the dark.

My heart was still in pain. My mind kept going back to my father.

After a moment, the biker turned his head to look at me through the corner of his right eye. "Look, I'm sorry about what happened. After we call the police and they sort this out, we'll go back there and bury our fathers. Everything will be better then."

"I don't believe you," I said through gritted teeth. The last thing I wanted right now was to start bonding with him, even if he was hot and my type. I never told anyone about this, but I liked bad boys more than I liked admitting that to myself.

Not to mention that his body was very warm when I was hugging him from behind.

"Believe me or don't, I know that everything will be better. You think I'm not in pain that they killed my father?" He said. "I'm going to get my revenge, one way or the other. I'll find out who did that and who ordered the attack, and then I'll kill every last one of them."

I believed him when he said that. I believed that he was going to seek revenge when he was feeling better.

He sped through another red light as I started to feel a strong scent in the air. Then, seconds later, I started to hear the rumbling of the motorcycle's engine. I snapped my head to look behind my shoulder as I realized that it was one of the Bear Bikers that was coming for us.

He twisted the handlebars of his motorcycle and it accelerated toward us. I was going to warn Cogwyn when he snapped his head to return his attention to the road in front of us.

"I saw him. Don't worry. I'm going to lose him."

Without thinking about it twice, I threw my arms around his body and hugged him tightly. He didn't say anything as he sped up the motorcycle and took us as far away from the pursuing biker as he could.

His motorcycle was trembling underneath us and, alongside Cogwyn, it was the only thing making me feel as safe as I could feel.

He swerved to the right and then to the left, entering another street. "How long until we get home?" I asked, raising my voice so that it could be heard through the rumbling of the motorcycle. I still didn't know what its name was, but I was pretty sure that he had named it. Every biker did that.

"Not much longer-" he was saying when a shot came from behind us, his body twitching for a second. I snapped my head up, wondering what just happened. Then, I started to feel something warm and liquid pooling on my chest.

Moments later, pain was flooding my body and I started to lose strength. My vision was darkening and I had no idea what was happening. All I knew was that Cogwyn was still riding us on his motorcycle and accelerating it as much as he could while also trying to lose our pursuer.

He swerved the motorcycle to the left, snapping his head to look over his shoulder. "I heard a shot. Are you feeling okay? Your arms are moving away from me. You need to hold on tight-"

Just as he was saying that, I couldn't keep doing what I was doing any longer. I couldn't keep hugging him. My body was losing strength and my vision was still getting darker.

Cogwyn started to slow down the motorcycle as he realized what was happening. I saw his eyes going wide as he noticed that I was falling off the motorcycle. It was still going pretty fast across the road and I knew that if I fell off of it, I'd die or get badly hurt.

"Bren!" He yelled, his hand snatching mine and yanking me back to the motorcycle. I could feel the rising pain in my chest, just underneath my heart. They could have killed me then. I didn't know why the Bear Bikers were still chasing us, but they were.

The rumbling of motorcycles' engines grew louder, now coming from all directions behind us. I looked over my shoulder and realized that more bikers were coming for us this time.

They looked determined, hungry, and were even transforming. They were between being humans and bears now. They couldn't keep riding their motorcycles if they finished their transformations. They would only transform if they needed to fight hand-to-hand.

"I'm not letting you fall off the bike," Cogwyn yelled, speeding up his motorcycle as the wind blew my hair behind my head. I was happy that he was gripping my hand so tightly and could still keep riding his motorcycle as if nothing bad was happening.

When it came down to it, it was obvious that he'd been in this kind of situation before. He was used to it.

"I'm going to take a shortcut. There's a place where we can hide and I can patch you up," he said, taking the left, entering an alleyway, and then another and one more. Before long, I couldn't hear or smell the bikers that had been chasing us.

I was pretty sure that they were still searching for us, but right now we should be okay. The motorcycle was gliding across the alleyway, stopping when we reached a building. It looked rundown, and it had broken windows and the paint was cracking and flaking off the walls.

Cogwyn turned off the engine of the motorcycle, wrapping one arm around me and pulling me off of it. "You might not like me and that's fine, but right now, I'm the only one who can help you."

He took me off the bike, his hand going for his pocket as he palmed it. "Shit, looks like I even forgot my phone in the church. I suppose they also didn't let you in with yours, right?" He asked, making me remember that a couple of workers did take care of the place.

They were probably dead now.

I shook my head, my vision going completely dark this time as I lost my consciousness. The only hope I had of pulling through this was this wolf shifter actually being more than who he appeared to be.

And I hoped that his intentions were really good.

CHAPTER 4

Cogwyn

He took a shot to his stomach and was bleeding pretty badly. I dragged him up to the second floor of the building, opened the door, laid him down on the bed, and then looked out the window to make sure that nobody was coming here.

The alleyway where the building was located was silent and peaceful, a page of a newspaper flying in the wind.

I closed the window, turned on the fan, and then started to patch up his wound. Bren didn't know this, but I used to go to medical school before dropping out of it and becoming a biker. A lot of things happened since then and I didn't want to remember them. I was just happy that I knew how to treat a wound as serious as his.

He was bleeding so bad I was worried he wasn't going to pull through. I had a first-aid kit tucked in one of the dressers. I only came to this building when I had a lot on my mind and needed to think about things.

I opened the first-aid kit, grabbed everything that was in it, and then started to dress his wound after taking out the bullet.

He groaned, turning around in the bed as I noticed that I was going to have to change the bedsheets. Blood was soaking them red. I checked his pulse and was happy that it was still strong. Even though Bren bled a lot, I was confident he had a good chance of pulling through.

Still, I was worried now and still thinking about my father. I fisted my hand as I promised myself again I was going to get my revenge, no matter what happened.

I pushed that thought out and focused on the matter at hand. I looped the gauze dressings around his torso, turned him around, and then checked his pulse again to make sure it was still strong.

After determining that it was, I pulled a chair over and plopped down on it, and started to look at Bren with no particular intention in mind. I was just gazing at him, time passing, and I was happy that he was feeling better. I wouldn't say that he was already okay, but there was no denying that the ointments I applied on his wound and the gauze dressings were already working their magic.

I jumped off the chair when I heard a motorcycle's engine speeding up far from here. It was probably one of the Bear Bikers who was hunting in the area for us. I was feeling pretty safe where I was.

It was unlikely they would find this place. This part of the city was always dark, filled with alleyways after alleyways, narrow roads, and other gangs that controlled it.

Dammit. If only I had my phone with me – or his phone – I'd be calling my mates to help me with this. They'd come running over here as fast as they could and they'd put those bikers back in their place. They needed to be killed – all of them.

I groaned, checking Bren out. No denying that he was cute and a sight for sore eyes, especially when he was sleeping. The biggest problem with him was that he was always a snobby asshole.

He always thought that he was better than most people just because he was more educated, more intelligent, and more 'cultured,' or whatever that was supposed to mean.

My body was relaxed on the chair, sunk in it. My clothes were soaked in sweat. Time passed and all I was doing was to keep looking at the Omega on the bed.

It felt good to be gazing at him like this when I knew he didn't know I was doing that. After all, I didn't want him to find out I thought he was cute.

I closed my eyes and when I reopened them, he was already sitting up on the bed. Supporting himself with his arms, he glanced at me, his eyes going wide.

Then, his hand started to palm the gauze dressings on his torso.

"You got shot in the stomach, but I think you're going to be okay. I don't have my phone with me and I'm not going out and risk getting caught. We need to stay here for the time being."

For a moment, Bren didn't say anything. He was staring at me and the way he was doing that was making me feel uncomfortable. It was like he never thought I'd help him as much as I did.

"You dressed my wound and saved me."

I nodded, smiling softly. "I did those things." After a moment of silence, I said, "and I'm expecting at least a thank you."

He pursed his lips, looking away from me. Well, Bren was never going to stop being the person I knew he was. Always snobby, always looking down on people like me, and always thinking that I was nothing more than a criminal.

I wasn't going to deny I did some things considered illegal, but I was also much more than that.

And here our parents were thinking we were fated mates and that we were going to get married like they did. We were so different. He preferred spending most of his time studying, locked up in his room, and pretending that the rest of the world didn't exist. Meanwhile, I was all about the thrills and making the most out of my life.

"Being grumpy like that isn't going to help us. We need to wait it out."

He pushed himself off the bed, standing up and losing his balance right after that.

"I'm not going to stay here another second with you," he

grumbled as he fell into my arms after I leaped from the chair where I was sitting.

Bren could be as grumpy as he wanted to be, but it wasn't going to change who I was. I was going to help him and then I was going to drop him off at his house, and that was going to be the end of it. After that, I needed to bury my father and then avenge his death. Just thinking about it, I felt my heart tight.

"Whoa there, Bren. You're not ready to go out yet. You can't even get off the bed. Your body is in pain and you know it."

He looked away, pushing himself off of me. He lied on the bed and started to stare at the ceiling.

"This is like my worst dream becoming real. I'm in the same room with you, I can't leave the building, and you helped me even though you didn't need to. It's like you're trying to tell me you are much more than the biker who hurts other people."

A moment later, I decided to ignore that.

I shook my head, stepping away from him. I opened the door to the bathroom, turned on the faucet, and I was happy when water started to come out from the showerhead. At least we had running water in the building.

"You can thank me later when you're feeling better. You know, I think I prefer it when you are sleeping more and talking less."

Bren grunted, crossing his arms over his chest and then turning around so that his back was facing me. I shook my head, took off my clothes, closed the door of the bathroom, and then stepped under the showerhead.

The water running around my body was already making me feel a lot better. I started to soap myself up and then I applied shampoo to my hair, not thinking about anything that didn't involve avenging my father.

I rinsed my body with the water and then stepped out from under the showerhead. I dried my body with the towel and then threw my clothes back on.

I opened the door to the bedroom again and I wasn't surprised when I found out that Bren was still with his back turned to me.

And here I was hoping he was going to change and become someone better. It looked like he was helpless when it came to that. He was always going to be grumpy and snobby.

And then, I heard a slight snoring coming from him. He was sleeping, which relieved me. It meant that he wasn't going to try to flee from the building when we weren't ready yet. We still needed to wait until the Bear Bikers got tired of hunting for us.

Bren was sleeping in the only bed we had. That meant I only had the chair to take a nap on, and knowing that didn't bother me. I had slept in worse places.

CHAPTER 5

Bren

I cracked my eyes open as I realized I was still in the same room, my heart tight even though I had no idea why. I sat up on the bed as I looked around and noticed that light streaks were coming through the window. It was the only window in this old, dusty room.

The smell in it was horrible, making me feel terrible. Not even the Alpha's scent was strong enough to make being in this place more bearable.

He was seated on the chair by my side, almost like he was trying to prove to me he cared about my wellbeing. It didn't matter that he dressed my wound. He wasn't going to fool me. Cogwyn was still the same asshole who used to bully me when I was in school. He was a couple of years older than me.

But that was just one of the many reasons why I didn't like him.

It was morning and I was already feeling much better, even though I didn't want to admit that it was thanks to him. I pushed myself off the bed and then started to walk on my tiptoes to the door. I wrapped my hand on the doorknob, pushed it open, and then looked over my shoulder.

Was I really going to do this? I asked myself, realizing that I was abandoning the only person who was helping me since the attack.

Sure, he would never stop being the asshole he was, a criminal who did the most unspeakable things, but he was still my only chance at getting home safely.

What was I going to do in this neighborhood, where everyone was Betas and they didn't like Omegas like us? I didn't know how to ride his motorcycle, even though I could try to learn on the fly. Not to mention that his motorcycle's key was probably in his pocket…

If I went over to him slowly and carefully, there would still be a good chance he would hear me. I was light, but not like a feather.

I groaned softly, closing the door when his eyelids opened slowly. Oh, fuck. Cogwyn was already waking up. He was going to see that I was trying to flee and mock me for not going through with it. It was going to be just like in school. He was going to say that I didn't have the courage to do it.

I sped over back to the bed on my tip-toes, hiding the fact that part of me felt thankful that he helped me. And also hiding one more thing which couldn't come to light, no matter what happened – Cogwyn was such a hottie! Even back in school, I thought that way about him.

He was my type. When I fell into his arms that time, I melted in them and, for a moment, I couldn't think about anything that didn't involve him holding me like that, telling me that everything was going to be okay. That was something that only bad boys like him could do.

Cogwyn pushed himself up off the chair, noticing me. I straightened up my spine as I smiled from ear to ear, trying to make it look like I wasn't doing what I was.

"You weren't trying to escape, or were you?" He probed, marching toward me. He was much bigger and taller than me. His fur was growing back, his eyes turning yellow as the shape of his pupils changed. He checked me out from bottom to top, disdain in his eyes. "And here I've been doing everything in my power to make you feel better. I should just kick you out to the Bears."

I whimpered, scurrying away from him as fast as I could. His muscles appeared to be growing bigger, harder, and his tattoos seemed to be getting stretched.

When I felt my butt touching the wall, I knew I didn't have any more room to wriggle around and escape from Cogwyn. He had me cornered.

And yet, I knew that he wasn't going to hurt me.

His fur went back into his body and his pupils returned to their normal shape. Sitting on the bed, he looked at me and made a movement with his hand, asking me to sit there with him.

"You don't have to like me and I'm not asking that you do, but we still need to help each other. Here. Come here. There's a lot we need to talk about."

Maybe it was his strong and intense Alpha scent that was doing it, but I started to step over to him slowly. I almost felt like the distance between us was growing larger.

Eventually, I sat on the bed as he repeated, "I know we don't like each other, but we need to work together."

And the way he said that made me feel that he was being genuine about it. Still, it was difficult for me to take him seriously, even though I knew the gravity of our situation well.

I couldn't help but feel something for him which I was assuming was connected to the fact I was an Omega. His scent was strong and very intense, drawing me to him. He took a shower last night and was smelling very nice this morning. He didn't even spray on perfume, but his smell was still exactly what I thought it was going to be after a hot shower.

"I'm trying to do that…" I mumbled, leaning toward him even though I knew I shouldn't be doing that. After all, what was he planning on doing now? Was he going to hurt me? And why was I even thinking that after he dressed my wound?

Truth was that he was hot, was being very caring with me right now, and was pretty much pushing every button that turned me on. It was like time was moving in slow motion for me as my head neared his head, his eyes locking with my eyes, my lips parting, and then… I realized the weight of what was happening.

At that moment, I jumped off the bed and strode away from him. I crossed my arms around my chest as I mumbled, "We're going to help each other out as much as we can, but no more than that."

A moment passed and Cogwyn didn't say anything, letting silence fill the void between us. He knew what happened and he wasn't stupid. He knew that we were almost kissing. He straightened up his spine, showing me that he was also leaning into me for a kiss.

That realization made me widen my eyes right away. Did that mean he also found me hot? That couldn't be. Cogwyn had been with several Omegas in his life and I was just one of many.

Not to mention that I couldn't be his type. He always said that I thought I was better than everyone else and was a snobby asshole.

After a while, he said, "Should we go out now? I think we should be in the clear."

I looked around and remembered that I was going to have to hug him from behind again, and that thought made me not want to go out with him right now.

I bit my lower lip, saying, "I think I want to wait a little while longer."

"And you want to stay in this dump for a couple more minutes with me?" He asked, crossing his arms over his chest as he looked down on me. "I thought you were beyond that. I mean, you've always said that the last thing you wanted to do is to live in a place like this for more than a day."

I whirled around, meeting his eyes. I thought I was going to see the eyes of someone who hated me, but I was seeing the opposite. I supposed that was because we were going through the same thing.

Both of our fathers died yesterday and we were still trying to cope with that. Not to mention that we were finally sharing another room that wasn't a classroom.

"This isn't about that. I've changed. I'm not the same person."

"Of course you aren't. You can't wait until the moment you don't have to spend another second with me."

"You know what?" I barked, raising my voice. "I'm not staying here another minute. I'm not staying here because you're being an asshole even though you don't have to be. I didn't give you any reasons to be like that to me." I threw the door open and stormed out of the room, eventually reaching the stairs and then the door out of the building.

Moments later, I felt a hand snatching me up and putting me on a motorcycle.

CHAPTER 6

Cogwyn

When I realized what was happening, it was already too late. One of the Bear Bikers, Dyson, popped out of nowhere and snatched Bren before I even knew what was happening. One moment he was outside the building and the next he was riding away on a motorcycle.

I stormed out of the building and stood where I was, frozen in place. I was helping Bren because I felt sorry for him, but then I realized it meant something more. I felt something more for him, like we really were fated mates.

I shook my head, rushed over to Desire, sat on it, and then rode off after them. My heart was in my throat. I shouldn't even be doing this.

It wasn't that I only thought of myself most of the time, but that I felt something for Bren that made me jealous for him.

As usual, I didn't put on my helmet as I didn't think it was necessary and I didn't like it. This time, though, I was doing it also because I needed to catch up to the other biker as soon as possible.

If I didn't do that, I had no idea what would happen to Bren. He needed my help and I was willing to risk my life to provide it.

Moments later, when I was speeding up my motorcycle, I finally spotted them in the distance. They were far from me, but not impossible to reach. I twisted the handlebars of the motorcycle, accelerating it to its limits. The engine was rumbling and the motorcycle itself was trembling, but I knew it was going to be okay.

When I was about to reach them, Dyson turned his head and pulled out his shotgun. It was a sawed-off shotgun, and he pulled the trigger with the gun right above Bren's head.

I thought about what was going to happen and how loud the shotgun was going to be, and my heart was tighter all of a sudden because I couldn't do anything to stop him.

But there was at least one thing I could try to do to help the Omega. "Bren!" I shouted, being loud enough to be heard through the engines of the motorcycles. "Cover your ears and duck. He's going to shoot."

"What?" He squeaked and even though I wasn't able to hear what he said, I knew that's what came out of his mouth. He was holding on tightly to Dyson but as soon as he realized he was pulling up his shotgun, he obeyed me, ducking and covering his ears with his hands.

I swerved to the right as I had just about enough time to judge where the bullets were going to hit. Most of all, right now I was worried for his safety. Bren was feeling better, but he still needed to rest.

I cursed Dyson for showing up. He always thought he was my nemesis. I always looked down on him because he was always nothing more than a nuisance. This time, he was pissing me off. It was like he was stealing Bren from me.

I was more surprised than anything I was feeling this way about it. After all, the old me would have already given up on him and let him be captured by the Bear Bikers.

The bullets hit the pavement and I had just about enough time to escape them, and also enough time to pull out my pistol and point it to Dyson's head. I didn't feel anything as I approached them on my motorcycle and pulled the trigger.

Dyson didn't have enough time to react. His hands let go of the motorcycle's handlebars, the motorcycle itself swerving left and right crazily. I threw my arm around Bren's body and pulled him to me. Dyson's motorcycle lost its balance, flipped across the pavement, and I put the Omega on the backseat.

After riding for a couple of minutes as he wrapped his arms around my chest and buried his head on my back, I finally pulled over when I felt that nobody was chasing us anymore.

Dyson had always been like that. He preferred to work on his own whenever he could. This time, I felt that he was doing that because the leader of the Bear Bikers told them to spread out throughout the neighborhood.

When I pulled over and turned off the engine of the motorcycle, I eased up my body and let out a sigh. I peeked behind my shoulder, loving the fact that Bren was still holding on so tightly to me. It was like he was telling me, even though he didn't mean to, that I was the only person who could make him feel safe right now.

That moment when we almost kissed… It was still in my mind even though he did what he did moments later. He said those awful things to my face, treating me like I was less than trash.

The old me would be dumping his ass right now and forgetting about his existence, especially now that the Sphere of Revelations didn't exist anymore. We weren't even able to hear what it was going to say, if we were fated mates or not.

When the Omega couldn't hear the rumbling of the motorcycles' engines anymore, he looked up and pushed himself away from me. I just realized that my fur was growing and that my teeth were getting bigger.

There were so many times when I couldn't control my transformation. I didn't want to let it happen because I always lost control of myself when it happened.

"What even happened?" He asked, and he was feeling so much fear I could hear his heart pounding in his chest.

"I just saved you again. That's what happened," I said, tucking my pistol back in the holster.

He blinked twice, pushing himself away from me further and getting off the bike. As he walked away from me, I asked him, "Are you going back to your house on your own? Do you really want to put a big target on your Omega father's head? Do you want to live with that?"

Bren stopped in his tracks, turning his head to look at me.

"If you are baiting me to stay another day with you, forget it. It's not going to happen."

"You say that like I'm not aware of it." I sighed, getting off my bike and marching toward him. When I stopped in front of him, I realized yet again I was much taller than him. "The truth is that you shouldn't go back to your house. I just realized that doing so would be a mistake. We don't even have news about what happened – if anything happened – in his house. By now, he probably already knows that his husband is dead."

Bren parted his lips and I thought he was going to say something when, suddenly, he threw his arms around me and hugged me tightly, burying his head in my chest.

"I just hate all this. I hate the fated mates thing. I hate the bear bikers, I hate the wolf shifters, and I hate you."

I was taken by surprise by what he did, but eventually I was used to it. I wrapped my arms around his body and hugged him as well. I didn't say anything, just letting Bren whimper and cry against my chest. If it was making him feel better and helping him cope with what happened, then I was feeling better, too.

It was the first time I was feeling so connected to him. We lived such different lives I thought this moment would never happen. It took our fathers dying on the same night to make me better understand what was going on in his mind.

When he pulled back, but without taking his arms off of me, he locked his eyes with me and I knew that this was the moment where he was thinking the same thing I was.

I moved my right hand over his spine, entangling my fingers in his hair. I pulled his head up and we connected our lips, washing away all the bad memories we were collecting since our fathers died. His lips were very sweet, just like I always thought they were. The truth was, I had always had a little crush on him.

And now I was fulfilling that crush by kissing him. He melted in my arms, moaning into my mouth. I slid my tongue between his lips and then pulled him more tightly against me, needing to feel his body and how warm it was.

Our tongues battled for control for a couple of minutes until I won the battle, letting a moment of nothingness pass so that he could catch his breath.

And when he locked his eyes with me again, I knew that things were taking a turn for the better between us.

CHAPTER 7

Bren

I never thought I'd kiss him and much less take him to my home. Even though he was right when he said that the Bear Bikers would have come here for my other father, they didn't.

I opened the door of my room for Cogwyn, opening my mouth when I was going to offer him some food. But he just lifted his hand, going to the bathroom.

"I'm going to take a shower first."

I didn't need to invite him to do that because he was always pushy like that. He opened the door of the bathroom and then closed it behind him, almost like this was his bedroom.

Even though I never thought he would ever take a shower in my own house, I was happy that he was. When I thought about it, I just couldn't deny the growing feeling in my heart that I was beginning to like him – and I was making sure I was stressing out that it didn't involve anything more than that.

After all, we kissed and it was just a moment where we needed to wash away all the bad things that were in our minds. Seated on the bed, I kept moving my hand over the bedsheets as I remembered everything that happened between me and my father. My last words to him must have hurt him more than I thought they did at the time.

In the meantime, I had no idea what I was going to do next. I thought that I did the right thing by inviting Cogwyn to live with me for a little while, even though I knew it was unlikely he was going to accept it.

The sun was already setting behind the buildings and I knew that he was only going to sleep with me tonight because he didn't have another place to go to. I mean, he had that rundown building in that neighborhood, but I didn't think he was very fond of it.

Minutes later, when my eyes were closed, he opened the door of the bathroom and I noticed that he was shirtless, his towel wrapped around the lower part of his body.

I couldn't help but check him out from bottom to top, realizing that my Omega side was now speaking louder than my common sense. I shouldn't and couldn't get involved with him. I knew it would only bring pain.

Cogwyn was rubbing his hair with a towel as he went over to the dresser, where I had said I had left some clothes for him. I had no idea if he was going to choose to wear them, but they were better than the worn clothes he had with him. They were smelly and even though I didn't like them at all, I couldn't help but admit that I wanted to take a sniff of them one day, if I ever found myself alone to do that.

After he finished rubbing his hair with the towel, he turned and walked over to me. I scooted away from him on the bed, and he noticed that. He stopped before sitting down on the mattress, and I noticed the bed sagging as he put all his weight on it.

I was still moving away from him when he grabbed my hand, making me snap my head to look at his eyes. They were determined and intense eyes that were staring at me as if he was reading my mind.

"Do you want to talk about it?" He asked, the way he was gripping my hand feeling determined. I felt that, if I wanted to move my hand away from him, he wouldn't hesitate before showing me that he didn't accept that. Everything that I wondered about us was beginning to show me that it was true.

This big wolf shifter had the same feelings for me I had for him, and it was difficult for me to process that in my mind. Moments later, he finally eased his grip on my hand and I exhaled.

I supposed there was no point in pretending I didn't kiss him. I did and it was going to be something that was going to forever be in my mind.

"I don't think we should," I responded, looking at his eyes, but I held my gaze only for a fraction of a second. As an Alpha, he was dominating even when all we were doing was looking at each other and talking. As an Omega, I was always going to be submissive. Sometimes I was also rebellious, but most of the time, I was submissive.

"Why not? I know that a lot happened in our lives because of the attack – and believe me when I say I'm going to avenge our fathers – but you just showed me something I thought would never happen. You always showed me how much you hated me for being different, for not following in my father's footsteps."

Cogwyn was right. His father was one of the most influential CEOs in the country and one of the reasons why he was able to choose this lifestyle over following in his father's footsteps.

Without his money and the influence he had, he would probably have died in the biker gang's initiation process. I heard it was pretty rough.

I could smell his scent and that it was growing more intense as time passed. Likewise, my cock was growing bigger under my pants. I still had to take a shower myself and I knew I was a little smelly, but Cogwyn wasn't letting that stop him. I knew that he was naked and that the only thing preventing me from peeking at his cock was his towel.

I took a deep breath in, his arm wrapping around me as he pulled me in for a kiss. We were picking up from where we left off, I thought, melting in his embrace. My hand went for his thigh, and I slid it under the towel, feeling the smoothness of his skin.

I thought that kissing someone so despicable, a biker that

could become a wolf at will, would make me feel like puking, but it was the opposite that was happening.

Perhaps it was the tragic events that happened that were making this feel so much better. It was the only thing that made me feel like it all happened years ago, that I was already over it even though I didn't even bury my father yet.

He slid his tongue into my mouth, pushing me down against the bed. He climbed on top of me, his hand pulling my shirt up as I grabbed his arms. Our eyes locked as he asked, "You don't want to do this anymore?"

I bit my bottom lip, finally answering, "It's not that. It's just that…"

He widened his eyes slightly. He was realizing something about me I had always kept under wraps. I just didn't want anyone to find out about it until the time was right.

"Don't tell me that you are…" He mumbled, making my heart speed up. I thought that he was going to jump away from me and walk out of my house, but he was still there when I reopened my eyes after closing them.

And then, his lips were connecting to mine again.

"That's so silly. I love it that you are that way," he purred, his muscles bulging as he started to feel my body with his hands. He had just finished taking off my shirt and I felt exposed that I was naked before him, time passing slowly. I loved that time was cooperating with us right now.

As he moved, the towel slid off of his body and finally revealed to me what I had been thinking about this whole time. It was all happening so suddenly and I was falling in love with him so quickly it was unbelievable that things were happening this way.

My eyes darted down to his cock and I drew in a short breath when I saw just how big it was. Not just big, but also thick and mean. It was hot, hard, and pointing right at me.

He was cut like I was, a smile flashing on his face as he realized that what was happening was already beyond our control.

He moved his hand up, pinched my nipple, and then started to work to take off my belt. Moments later, when I was already past trying to stop this, he took off my belt and started to lower my pants.

I pushed him away from me – or at least, I tried to – as I realized I hadn't done something very important, but it appeared that he was reading my mind just like I thought he was going to.

He lowered his head, murmuring into my ear, "Don't worry, Bren. I closed the door."

CHAPTER 8

Cogwyn

My heart was pounding in my head as I realized the weight of what was happening. I was kissing this Omega, finally doing something with him I thought would never happen. I just finished taking off his pants and now it was time to take off his underwear, too. He had a pair of dark boxer briefs on, and underneath it I could see the shadow that his cock made. It was a little on the small side, but I thought it was perfect for me.

I kissed Bren again, groping his chest and feeling his perfect little abs. I moved my hands down, ripped off his boxer briefs, and then grabbed his cock. Just one hand was enough.

My teeth were growing pointier and I knew that the other side of me wanted to come out. I pushed him back, keeping him away from this. I was going to knot this rebellious Omega and he was going to be mine, no matter what happened.

I was in his house and everything should be fine here. I thought that the Bear Bikers had already mounted an attack against this place but, thankfully, that didn't happen.

I kicked those thoughts out of my mind as they didn't have any place in here right now. I could hear his raggedy, uncontrolled breathing. Bren was finally, for a couple of minutes, not the up-tight asswipe he'd always been. Hell, he even looked like a completely changed person himself.

I had this uncontrollable urge to knot him and it wasn't even popping up in my mind that I should probably wear a condom. I was just devouring his neck with impossible, long kisses, feeling the warmth of his body and how it was everything I wanted right now.

I was going to knot this Omega and nothing was going to stop me.

I stroked his dick for what felt like hours, his body squirming and convulsing when he orgasmed. His milk came out in long, hot ropes all over his body, some of them even hitting my belly. I lowered my head and lapped them up. I scooped up his jelly on my belly with my finger and then brought it to my mouth, licking it.

"It's wonderful, and you're delicious," I groaned, moving over his body and going down on his dick. I enclosed my lips around his little cockhead, giving the underside of it long and controlled licks that brought him over the edge again. Bren grabbed my hair however he could, grinding his body against mine as he convulsed again and again. I almost thought he was going to pass out, but it didn't happen.

He was still right here with me and I was holding his head, sweat pooling on his forehead.

"Do that again, please," he murmured, his lips brushing over mine when he attempted to kiss me again. I could only do what he was requesting of me, his hand going for my dick and grabbing it. He gave it a couple of strokes, his eyes wide when he realized how big I was.

I pecked his neck one more time and he threw his legs around my body, pinning me down against him. I groaned into his mouth, rubbing my balls against his nuts as I felt that familiar sensation that preceded an orgasm. But I wasn't going to climax until the right moment.

My nails were growing bigger, the transformation happening despite my efforts. I could only knot him when I was inside of him, so I didn't worry that anything I didn't like was going to happen.

I moved down over his body again, playing with his balls as he threw his head backward, coming for the third time in a row. This time, his hot and creamy sperm hit all over my face, and I scooped up everything I could with my fingers. I licked them off one by one, my eyes locked with my Omega's.

That turned him on, his cheeks redder. I gave his ballsack a little tug and then turned him around. He was already wet and clenching for me, just waiting for me to penetrate him. As the good-natured Alpha I was – I chuckled at that thought – I lapped up his juices and then grabbed his thighs.

I pulled him to me slowly, lining up my dick to his tunnel before nudging it. Moments later, I thrust in with greater force and then penetrated him. I slid in all the way, bottoming him out.

When I was all the way inside of him, seeing only my balls right now, I lowered my head and murmured into his ear, "Does it hurt too much?"

He shook his head, giving me the okay to go on. I started to roll my hips, my hands holding his body over the bed. I was letting time pass so that he was used to my size. Meanwhile, he was clenching me tightly and I knew that I'd only pull out of him after coming and impregnating him.

The thing about us being fated mates was just a mere memory in my mind right now, and I didn't give it much thought. I focused on pounding in and out of him slowly, picking up speed when I realized that he was much better used to my size.

My dick grew bigger, my balls slapping off of his asscheeks when I could feel my sperm coming out. When it exploded and orgasm swept through my body, I dug my fingers deeper into his thighs and pulled him more tightly against mine.

I knotted the Omega.

My dick throbbed and erupted inside of his tunnel, the thought that I was getting him pregnant feeling so right – even though we didn't plan for this and it would be unlikely he wouldn't hate me after this.

Minutes later, my orgasm faded when my shaft returned to its normal size. My body was sated and now it felt that I could finally pull out of him. And so I did that, plopping down on the bed as he did the same thing.

Bren had his back turned to me and, for a moment, while my dick was still getting softer, I thought something bad had happened. Maybe he was finally realizing that he didn't want to get pregnant and that I was an asshole for doing that.

I put my arm around him and pulled him to me, his eyes looking at me as I realized that tears were coming out of them. I slid my hand over his cheek, asking, "Something happened? You look distressed."

"I think… my father might have been right about it. We were made for each other, weren't we? We are fated mates. That's what the sphere was going to tell us."

I was caressing his cheek when I said, "Hey, no need to cry right now. I know what happened and what it means to you. I don't know what the sphere would have said, but I think it's irrelevant right now anyway. You just showed me a side of you I thought you didn't have. You showed me that you aren't just the snobby asshole I always thought you were."

Bren chuckled. "Thanks… I think I want to say that I'm beginning to like you."

He was still having difficulty breathing, his chest expanding and contracting slowly and noticeably. I pulled him more tightly against me, my dick already hard as I thought about fucking him again.

I knew that it wasn't going to happen – at least, not right now – but the thought was still in my mind, and my mind could always be changed.

"That's much better than who you were like before. I felt like you could have slit my throat while I was sleeping."

"For a good reason. You were always putting me down when

we were younger."

"Well, now we're grownups and we know better than doing that, don't you agree?" I brushed my lips against his lips again, biting his upper lip for a fraction of a second. He moaned, pushing his body closer against mine. I was so surprised by the way he was taking this I thought he never would.

"So, how was it like, losing your virginity with me?" I quizzed, just holding him against me and really feeling like we were fated mates, just like that dumb sphere was going to tell us.

"It was amazing," he crooned, snuggling up on me as we cuddled and fell asleep. I never said this to Bren, but it was the best sleep I had in a while. I couldn't help but feel impatient about what the future held in store for us, despite all the other bad things that came with that attack.

I still needed to find out everything about it, even though I was already looking forward to a life together with Bren.

CHAPTER 9

Bren

I was in his arms when I woke up, turning to the right in the bed as I noticed the photo of my parents on the nightstand. One of my fathers – the one that survived and was still living in our house – didn't approve of Cogwyn at all.

I always felt connected to him and that I could understand him, but now that I was in Cogwyn's strong arms, I couldn't look at him the same way. I couldn't help but think he was the Alpha I didn't even know I was looking for.

I sighed, not wishing to turn this into an argument I couldn't win. Ranulf was a good man, but even the night before he already told me that he didn't want Cogwyn to spend another night in our place.

I told him that I understood why he said that, but now that it was the next morning and the sunlight was shining brightly through the windows, I couldn't help but wonder if maybe he couldn't be convinced otherwise.

I fisted my hand, thinking about my dead Alpha father. If Ranulf was there, he'd be dead right now too, and I would never have forgiven myself. I should be happy that he was here and alive. At least we could mourn together.

We still needed to go over the procedures involving the burial of our fathers, and I could already tell that it wasn't going to be pretty. One of the reasons for that was that Ranulf wasn't going to think twice before spouting that he didn't want Cogwyn's father to be buried near his husband.

Either way, I never thought that was going to happen anyway. Cogwyn was going to choose a different cemetery for his father's final resting place.

I was going to make sure that I was going to be there for him regardless, though. He deserved that much from me.

I picked up the portrait with all three of us in it, brushed my finger over the photo, and then shimmed out of Cogwyn's heavy arms. He groaned, turning so that his back was facing me.

I still couldn't believe that I lost my virginity to my bully. He was so incredible. I thought that it was going to happen with my boyfriend, but he'd always been postponing it. I didn't know why, but he never looked forward to us having sex.

I got off the bed and then went to the shower, still stealing glances at the huge man in my bed. Did he knock me up and did that mean I was going to have his baby – or many? I didn't know, but I was still under the effects of the fact that I lost my virginity and I couldn't be any happier. I'd only be happier if that attack hadn't happened.

Perhaps my father had always been right about one thing – some things always happened for a reason. I didn't want to think about it this way, but maybe the attack happened so that Cogwyn and I could learn we were different than who we thought...

I went to the shower room, opened the door, and then started to take a shower. As the water flowed around my body and then down to the drain, I was already feeling even better. I had sex with Cogwyn when I was smelly and dirty. I couldn't help but look forward to when we could do it when I was smelling better.

I chuckled at that thought as I walked out of the shower room, rubbing a towel on my hair until it was dry. I just finished putting on my clothes when I heard a groan coming from the bed. I snapped my head to it as I realized that Cogwyn was waking up.

Even though I still had to explain to Ish that things between us were going to be different from now on, I was really looking forward to having many mornings like this one in the future.

It would be magical to wake up in his arms almost every morning, to kiss his lips even when things weren't going so well between us, and possibly to carry his baby in my belly.

"Good morning, Cogwyn. Do you want to stay for breakfast?" I asked him, noticing that he was still groggy after oversleeping. I did check the time on the clock on the wall and it said that it was already past ten in the morning.

We slept a lot because we were so tired last night. That was one of the many reasons why I convinced my Omega father that I wanted Cogwyn to sleep here.

He rubbed his eyes with his hands as he sat up on the bed. "Breakfast? Sure, love. I think I would like that."

Love? Wow.

I raked his body with my eyes as I said, "But first, I think you should get dressed."

He cracked open a smile, pushing the comforter away from his body as he got off the bed. I checked him out again as he went to where he had left his clothes, picked them up, and then put them on.

When he was finishing putting on his shirt and leather jacket, we heard someone rapping on the door. My eyes went wide when I realized it could only be a certain someone, and it was someone very important to me and very dear to my heart.

"Oh-oh," I said, going to the door and opening it. I wasn't surprised when I saw that it was my Omega father that had been rapping on the door. His eyes looked fierce and angry, like he was in the presence of something he despised so much he'd kill it if he could.

And by that I meant Cogwyn.

Ranulf glared over my right shoulder, finding the person he was looking for.

"I thought you had already left," he growled, stepping into the room and making his presence bigger than it was. Even though he was an Omega like I was, he was braver than most people thought he was. He thought he was just protecting me because he didn't think Cogwyn was the right man for me.

I knew why he was doing this and why he was thinking he was just protecting me, but I wasn't going to let him stand in the way of me and Cogwyn. Most of all, I wasn't going to let him sour this perfect moment I was sharing with him.

I leaped and stopped when I was in front of him, looking into his eyes as I realized he wasn't much taller than me.

"Could we just not do that now?" I begged him, hoping that he was going to understand me.

He sighed, saying, "Alright, I'm going to try to ignore him, and either way I came here for something else. We need to go and bury Parth, Bren. The police went there last night, picked up the bodies, and took them to the morgue."

I turned my head to look at Cogwyn, noticing that he was looking down. He was still also trying to process the news that his father was dead. I wished Ranulf could see what I was seeing, the pain in Cogwyn's eyes, and feel some empathy for him.

"And we should go there now after breakfast. They have some important news to tell us about the attack. They think they know why it happened."

As soon as he mentioned that, Cogwyn's eyes shot up. He hurried over to us, putting himself between me and Ranulf. "Did they tell you anything about it? Did they tell you why it happened?"

Ranulf narrowed his eyes and I could see that a vein in his neck was popping out. It didn't matter that he was much older than Cogwyn. He was still just an Omega like I was and, thus, he tended to be more submissive. He couldn't stand up to Cogwyn without going against what was in his nature.

He shook his head, responding, "No. Unfortunately, they didn't tell me anything." A tear broke out and rolled down his cheek. I could feel the pain he was feeling that his husband died. He wished he was there when it happened so that he could have stopped it. I doubted he would have been able to, but he still wished he was there.

Cogwyn tsked, striding to the door and marching into the hallway. As soon as I noticed it looked like he was going out, I went after him. He turned around, saying, "I don't think I have time for breakfast. Not today, anyway. Maybe some other time."

He turned around and strode out of the house, leaving me flabbergasted. I knew why he was in so much of a hurry. He wanted to make sure he was going to be there for his dead father in the morgue.

He wanted to make sure he was going to get what he needed as soon as possible because he had his vendetta to finish.

And thinking that, I couldn't help but feel that he was putting himself in danger when he didn't need to. I wanted revenge too, but he was alone in this.

Did I think that the other wolf shifters were going to help him with his vendetta? I didn't know, but I was going after him no matter what.

That's why, after glancing over my shoulder at my father, I took off after Cogwyn. I was going to stop him before he did something he'd regret later.

CHAPTER 10

Cogwyn

I was going to have my revenge and it didn't matter what happened from now on. First, I needed to go to the morgue to see my... dead father. I was just crossing out of the property when I heard footsteps coming from behind me hurriedly. I knew who they belonged to before I even turned around to see who it was.

As I turned around, I said, "Bren, I know we had an amazing night together, but I'm busy with something right now, and I think we should go to the morgue as soon as possible. Our fathers need us."

"I know that they do, but I want to go there with you."

Since waking up, I started to think about so many things. I started to think about what our relationship was going to lead to, the people that we were hurting because we were beginning to fall in love, and also that we were both pissing off our Omega fathers.

I knew what my other father thought of Bren and that he wasn't the right Omega for me. That was one of the many reasons why he didn't show up at the church.

I looked over his shoulder, noticing that his Omega father was staring at us from the doorway. He wished he could pull out a gun and shoot me dead right here, and he was not doing that because he didn't want to go to jail and make everything much worse.

I could feel the hatred he had for me and how it was swirling in the air. I could feel it in the way that it changed his scent, the way he kept his shoulders up and tense, and also the way his eyes were narrowed as he tried not to think about all the ways he could get rid of me.

I had a really amazing night with Bren and even though it was possible I got him pregnant, I couldn't help but wonder what our lives together would be like if he were to live with me.

He grabbed my hands, saying, "I'm going to end things with Ish and everything will be better. I want to stay with you."

As soon as he said that, I noticed his Omega father's shoulders pushing against his own body, like he was doing everything in his power not to spill out everything he was thinking right now.

I started to walk away, taking my hands off of his. "The more I stay in this place, the more I realize just how much your Omega father doesn't like me. He doesn't even feel sorry that my father was also killed in the attack."

Bren stopped in his tracks, exhaling. "I know he's having a hard time processing what happened, but he's a good person. I know that he'll come around one day, if you let him. Don't worry about him. Think about us."

I ran my hand over my face, thinking about my father and that I needed to find out what the police knew about the attack. I needed to find out everything they knew because I was going to use that information to finish my vendetta.

I just didn't have the time and the mind to think about our relationship right now, even though I knew very well that when we were making love and he was showing how much he wanted me, I promised myself I'd give ourselves a chance.

Well, that was then and things were different now.

I got on my bike when I realized that Bren was standing right by my side. I turned the handlebars of the motorcycle, firing up the engine.

"I'm going to the police station. If you want to come with me, you can, but I'm not going to stay another minute at your house.

It's very clear to me that I'm not welcomed here at all."

"Aren't you at least going to try to call your friends to help you with this? I'm sure they want to get involved."

I thought about it, but I just didn't have the time to tell my boss about the attack and that I was still alive. Gosh, so many things happened between then and now I didn't even remember, this whole time, that I was part of a gang who prided themselves on how we always helped each other out.

"As soon as I get there, I'll tell them." I sighed, looking ahead at the road. When I turned my head to him, I said, "For your safety, I don't think you should come with me. The Bear Bikers might attack us again. I'm pretty sure that they are still trying to kill you."

When I was going to ride away on my bike, Bren grabbed my hand again and stopped me. He was looking into my eyes, which was something he never did often, as he said, "I should be going there with you anyway. My father is also very important to me and, if there is someone who I want to do this with, then it's you."

I sighed, saying, "But first, I need to go to the morgue, and then I'll go and get some support."

He smiled, swinging his leg over the bike as he sat down. When he wrapped his arms around my body, I already felt better. I could already imagine us riding in the streets, the wind blowing against our faces. It was like we were always meant to make this happen and be together.

His father came rushing to us right away, putting himself in front of the bike. "Where do you even think you are going with Bren?"

"To the morgue and don't worry – I'm going to bring him back before the sun sets today."

He relaxed his shoulders, stepping away from the bike. "All right, but promise me that he'll be safe. I'm going to send some of my guards with you. They will follow you in their cars and make sure that you'll both be safe. I want to find out the truth about what happened as much as you do."

I nodded, realizing that we were finally agreeing on something. Hopefully, things were going to take a turn for the better between us. When I took off on my motorcycle, Bren buried his head in the crook of my neck as we went to the morgue.

He shifted his head slightly before asking, "Do you think we'll be okay together?"

"I'm sorry, what?" I asked, turning my head momentarily to glance at him.

He looked hurt by what I said, turning his head away.

Seconds later, when I realized he wasn't going to say anything else, I added, "What were you trying to say?"

He shook his head. "I don't think I want to talk about it anymore. You were so ready to leave me after we had that amazing night together."

"I'm not even sure what we are to each other anymore. I feel a strong pull to you, but I realize you're still much different than me and that we can't actually live together as a couple. I mean, are you going to want to live as a biker like me?" I asked him, studying his face to see what he thought about that.

"I was willing to do that, but it looks like you are the one who's not willing to change. I want to be with you for the rest of my life, even if that means fighting against the only father I still have."

I blinked twice, finding it hard to believe that he changed so much in so little time. Maybe it was his possible pregnancy that was changing him so much.

Either way, I didn't have time to think about building a family and having babies with him right now. I was aware that I thought differently last night, but things changed and I just wanted my revenge as soon as possible.

CHAPTER 11

Bren

I thought that he was going to say to me we were going to build a family and that everything was going to be fine between us. The thing I had with Ish was nothing more than a fling, now that I was thinking better about it. I never really loved him. Not the way I loved this man who I was sure had knocked me up.

We walked out of the morgue and his biker friends were already standing outside, their motorcycles rumbling under the sunlight.

The leader was an older man with pepper and salt hair, a long beard, and a mean stare. Just looking at him now was making me feel afraid of him, even though I knew I didn't have to be. After all, he was part of us now. He was going to fight for us to help Cogwyn with his revenge.

And don't get me wrong when I say that I wanted revenge as well, but not in the way Cogwyn was thinking it should happen. He wanted revenge by his own hands and to teach the bear bikers that they should never have messed with him.

I was afraid of that because I didn't want him to put himself further in danger than he already was. But looking up and finding his eyes, I could tell that he wasn't about to change his mind. If anything, now that he saw his dead father in the morgue, he was even more determined about going through with his plan.

"I'm sorry about what happened," the president of the gang said, uncrossing his arms.

"I know, and I'm not letting things end this way. We need to get one of them and get all the information we need out of him, no matter the cost. They started a war with us as far as I'm concerned.

"I don't think I can change your mind about that and, don't worry, we'll make it happen. I'm just curious about one thing right now, though," the older man said, his intense eyes glaring at me like I was some kind of pestilence. I thought that that was going to be enough to make Cogwyn stand up for me and make me feel welcomed in his gang – even though I was pretty sure there was no way that was going to happen – but that's not what he did. His shoulders were still tense and I could tell he was still thinking about just one thing – killing all the people involved in the attack, and it didn't matter if that involved killing all of the bear bikers and continuing their war. "Why is here still with you? I thought that his kind didn't mingle with us bikers."

"He's here because his father was also killed. Our fathers thought that we were fated mates and were going to use the Sphere of Revelations to prove that. We didn't have enough time for that, though."

"I see," the president said, glancing me over with disdain in his eyes. If it was up to him, he'd be kicking me out of here right at this moment. But since Cogwyn was by my side and my father's body-guards were with us, too, he wasn't going to do that.

But it was enough to make me feel even less welcomed in Cogwyn's world. He was right when he said that I wasn't going to become a biker and that I wasn't going to live like him.

And hell, if we were to have a child together, I didn't want him growing up in an environment that was about killing people and committing all kinds of other atrocities.

Even though Cogwyn was a better man than these people, our child would still be involved in all of that and I couldn't have that. We needed to have a definitive discussion about it and, hopefully,

I could change his mind about it. But looking up and finding the eyes of the man who might have knocked me up – I still needed to wait until I could take the pregnancy test – I wasn't sure I wanted to have that conversation with him anytime soon.

It wasn't something that I could run away from, though, I thought.

"We'll see you in the club later, sharp. You know the time of the meeting. Be there and don't be late. We'll mount an attack, find out what's happening with the Bear Bikers, and hopefully figure out what's going on. Don't worry. We'll sort everything out."

Cogwyn nodded and the other bikers took off, turning to the right when they disappeared behind the buildings. I glanced at Cogwyn, wishing I could read his mind so that I could make all of this much easier.

I sighed and grabbed his hand to get his attention. It worked. He was looking at me, but it appeared he was determined about something that didn't involve our relationship. It looked like he was thinking about something else, focused just on it.

"Cogwyn…"

"What?"

"I think we need to talk about it, don't you?"

"About us?" He groaned, a car driving behind him.

"Yes, of course we need to talk about ourselves, or do you want to make me think that all that happened doesn't mean anything anymore to you?"

He ran his hand over his face, looking stressed out. "It was just a one-night stand. Just take a pill or something so that you don't get pregnant."

I didn't say anything, just letting silence take hold of the atmosphere between us. He wasn't looking directly at me, which was something new coming from him. Cogwyn always looked at my eyes when he was worried about something.

He wasn't doing this because he wanted to, was he?

"No, it was more than that. You shouldn't lie to me. I know it was more than that, and I know it means a lot that you can finally understand what's going on in my mind."

"I don't actually understand you that much," he growled, fur growing on his body. I didn't think he was going to transform, but it was more than evident that what was happening was making him feel more stressed.

"You do. When you were inside of me, I could understand you and you could understand me." I sighed, letting a moment of silence pass so that he could better understand what I meant by that.

"And I'm not going to take any pills. If I end up having your child, then I'll be happy to take care of him or her."

He widened his eyes, stepping toward me hurriedly. "You can't be serious about that. You can't have my child because we are not even fated mates. We'll never know that for sure."

Cogwyn was right about that, but we didn't need to know if we were fated mates or not. What the Sphere of Revelations was going to say didn't matter anymore. What mattered was what we felt about each other, and it was the strongest thing I felt right now.

"It's my choice, don't you think? I can do whatever I want. I'm just disappointed that you changed your mind about us all of a sudden. I thought we were building toward something more meaningful. I thought you were finally changing and becoming someone better than the asshole biker you were."

There. I said it. I just felt that it needed to be said. This whole time, Cogwyn was being an asshole again, almost like he was trying to toss me away after using me.

He blinked twice, stepping away from me as he went back to his motorcycle. He grabbed the left handlebar as he said, "If I'm the asshole you think I am, then why do you still care about me?"

I stepped toward him, holding out a hand. It was like I was trying to reach out to him even though I knew it looked like he didn't want anything else to do with me. When I realized that, I lowered my hand and looked away. I hugged myself as I started to feel alone.

There was a moment of silence and, given the scent I could feel in the air, I was almost thinking he was beginning to regret the words he said to me.

"I hope you don't mean what you said. It hurt me more than I thought it would."

"Is there really no chance you could just drop your revenge and focus on building a life with me?" I asked, just wishing I could be holding his hand again.

He shook his head and didn't say anything. Moments later, he turned on the engine of the motorcycle and drove off, turning to the left when I couldn't see him anymore. I was left all alone on the sidewalk, wishing I could go back and reverse everything I said. I wished I could take it all back.

I turned and started to walk towards one of the cars that my bodyguards were driving. He opened the door and I sat down in the backseat, lowering my head and putting it on my hands. I was covering my face with my hands because I didn't want anyone to see it. I didn't want anyone to find out how much it hurt me. We just broke up even though we didn't even spend any time together, other than the night we shared in my bed.

And worse, the feeling that I got tossed away was growing stronger in my mind and it was beginning to make more sense than Cogwyn loving me.

Not to mention that if I was going to have his baby, then I was already beginning to feel happy that he or she would grow up in a much kinder environment, without the bikers and the violence that came with them.

"Do you want to go back home, master?" The bodyguard that was also the driver asked me, looking over his shoulder.

"Just take me wherever you want. I don't care anymore at this point," I barked, lying in the backseat as I wished I had someone to hold me tightly right now. I didn't just lose my father these last few days, but also the person who really connected with me in a way I had never felt before, which was one of the reasons why I now thought he was my fated mate.

The car was driving across the roads and I couldn't do anything that wasn't crying. If Cogwyn was still the same person I knew he was, he would be holding me in his arms right now and murmuring into my ear that everything was going to be fine. But it looked like I misjudged him. He went back to being his older self, who didn't care about anyone that wasn't himself...

I felt a hand nudging my shoulder as I flapped my eyelids open, realizing that Ranulf had opened the door of the car and was standing by my side, outside the vehicle.

"I knew he was going to leave you. I tried to warn you, but he was just using you. He's always been like that. Don't you remember anymore all the times when you came home from school crying because of him?" He asked when I sat up in the backseat, looking at his comforting eyes.

I nodded, saying, "You're right. You've always been right and I'm sorry I said the things I said to you."

As I got out of the car and the driver took it to the garage, Ranulf asked, "You didn't have sex with him when he was in your room, right?"

I knew why he was asking about that. He was worried I was pregnant with Cogwyn's baby.

I just shook my head and said, "No, it didn't happen. He just slept in my room, but he slept on the floor."

Ranulf studied my face for a fraction of a second, looking away as we crossed the main door into the main hall.

"Good. That means we don't have to worry about it."

CHAPTER 12

Cogwyn

Months later, I was still thinking about everything that happened. I left Bren because I couldn't stand his father, the environment where he lived, and all the people in his life who always thought so highly of themselves.

I was on my motorcycle, waiting for a certain asshole to show up. He was one of the Bear Bikers, stumbling out of the bar as he loosely held a bottle of beer. One of the other customers of the place kicked him out, shouting, "Get out of here and never come back."

He was so drunk he couldn't even finish his transformation. His irises changed their color, his nails popped out, but then, seconds later, he was already fully back to his human form.

I couldn't help but chuckle, getting off Desire and stepping toward him, measuring the weight of my footsteps because I didn't want to alert anyone about my presence. I was deep in Bear territory and if they got a whiff of me, there would be hell. I was doing this alone because more people involved in this assignment would only make things worse.

Not to mention that I needed to do this on my own anyway. The president and the rest of the Wolf Shifters were doing all they could – or at least they were trying to make me think they were – regarding the murder of my father, but I was pretty sure they could still be doing more. I was just disappointed in them was all.

I took the left when he entered an alleyway. The poor guy didn't even know where he was going, bouncing off a wall as he lost his balance and fell over on the ground. I was just behind him and I was going to do everything in my power to get as much information out of him as I could.

I knew the names of the people behind the attack and I was going to kill them, one by one. My fur was growing back on my skin as I tried to suppress my scent. I couldn't let the guy I was pursuing find out that I was coming for him, or any of the people who lived here in this neighborhood, for that matter. I didn't want more attention on me than I already had.

He turned his head to look behind his shoulder when he felt a presence looming behind him. "Who the hell are you and what are you doing here? You don't look like someone from the family," he said, crawling away from me.

"No, I don't, and I'm here for you and not for them. Do you remember Misk Garrett, the CEO of Wolfza?" I growled, hoping that my voice and the tone I was using were going to make him piss his pants.

"No, who's he?" He asked, his voice sounding slow, and it annoyed me every time he spoke. I grabbed him by the collar of his shirt and hoisted him, noticing that my nails were growing. I needed to control my transformation or else my scent was going to give away that I was here.

I studied his eyes, realizing that he was speaking the truth when he said that. He was just a low-level grunt of the gang and it was likely that he didn't even know what he was doing when he attacked me and my family.

"Think better about it. Think very carefully about that night when you tried to kill me." I stared into his eyes, giving him time to remember my face. When his eyes bulged, I knew that I finally had him where I wanted him.

"You are Cogwyn Garrett. We should've killed you when we

had the chance. My life turned into a living hell because of you."

Knowing that he was suffering because of me and the Wolf shifters was empowering. I took pleasure in that and I wasn't going to hide it, a smile showing up on my face.

"Good. You should be afraid of me and you should always remember my name and face." I shoved him against the wall of a building and he almost lost his consciousness, his eyes closing until I punched him against the wall again. "I want you to tell me everything you did that night. I want you to tell me why you attacked us. My father never did anything against you. He was just a businessman."

He turned his eyes slowly as he stared at me again. "I don't think I should tell you anything. You won't let me get out of this alive even if I do."

I felt my body growing bigger, my muscles straining against my clothes.

"Thing is, I don't think you have a choice. You either get a chance at escaping this by telling me everything you know, or I kill you right now and find someone else to extract the information I need."

He whimpered, throwing his beer bottle against me, but I slapped it away. It exploded on the ground into a million pieces, beer splashing out of it.

I shoved him against the wall again, my nails growing bigger as my skin started to be covered by my fur.

"Tell me everything you know. I'm not going to give you another chance."

"Alright, alright," he mumbled, taking a deep breath. "But if you think that you're going to like my answer and what I know, you'll be disappointed."

"Why is that?" I growled, wishing I could open a hole in his neck. I was going to do that as soon as I didn't need him anymore.

Thing was, I needed him now because he was the only idiot in the Bear Bikers who was alone sometimes. All the others always walked in groups and they also never got wasted like this guy was.

"I remember that you were in a relationship with a certain Omega by the name of Bren…"

I blinked, not understanding why he mentioned Bren all of a sudden. I was surprised that a guy like him knew about the beginning of a relationship that never really flourished.

"What do you know about him?" I asked, feeling that even after all this time, the mere mention of his name was enough to make me feel stressed out about the way things turned out.

"It was his father who ordered the attack. Your Omega fathers did. They never wanted you together. That's what happened."

When he said that, I eased my grip and he fell to the floor, scurrying away as soon as he could. I was paralyzed by his words and I had no reason to believe he lied. My Omega father and Bren's ordered the attack against us? It didn't even make any sense. Even though they knew each other, they never really talked.

When I turned my head to try and find that drunkard again, he was already gone and I was alone in the alleyway. I heard police sirens in the distance and I didn't think that they were coming this way.

Still, I decided to move away from there as fast as I could as I went back to Desire. I swung my leg over the motorcycle, turned on the engine, and started to ride away from there.

When I was out of the Bear Bikers' territory, I could finally try to process what I knew. If my Omega father was one of the parties who ordered the attack, then I needed to have a straight conversation with him.

I needed to look into his eyes to find out the truth. And then, I'd need to also talk to Ranulf and find out if I could dig out the rest of the truth.

The motorcycle screeched to a halt and I jumped off of it, storming into my apartment room. I was still trying to process everything that he said to me, my mind remembering the amazing night I had with Bren. Truth was, even after breaking up with him, he was always in my mind. I always thought of him, even when things were going well in my life.

Could it be that he really was my fated mate? I didn't know, but he still meant a lot to me and I had no idea if he got pregnant or not. We never talked again after we 'broke up.'

My mind was such a mess and now I needed to go and find out the truth about what happened.

CHAPTER 13

Bren

I was walking down the sidewalk when I started to hear the rumbling of a motorcycle's engine. I didn't think much of it, knowing that I lived in a city where bikers were everywhere. My hands were in my pockets, my head lowered.

Since breaking up with Cogwyn and then Ish, I hadn't been the same person. I tried pushing all the bad memories out of my mind, but I always kept thinking that something was wrong with me, especially after finding out that I was pregnant.

My belly was big now, but I knew it was going to grow even bigger. I put my hands on it, sliding them on it as I continued to walk across the sidewalk. I kept on ignoring the sound of the motorcycle's engine as I knew it couldn't be Cogwyn.

He left his mark on me and it was always going to be there.

I could still remember the night when he took my virginity and made me his. But the next day, he was already spouting out a lot of bullshit that we weren't going to work as a couple, that we should live separately, and that my life was better without him.

I shook my head, hating the fact that he said those things to me and I wasn't able to rebuke him. I was still trying to process everything that happened then.

I turned my head to the left when I heard the motorcycle pulling over. For a moment, I thought that it was a thug trying to rob me, but it was just a biker with his girlfriend, who was in the back-seat. It looked like she was an Omega like I was, and I had to say that the biker was hot himself.

I stopped walking just to admire them, but I immediately went back to what I was doing because I didn't want to come off as a creep.

I turned to the left, crossed the crosswalk, and then went toward where the bar I was looking for was. It was a dive bar located in the neighborhood where my house was, and from the reviews I saw on the Internet, it appeared to be good.

I heard a couple of rumbles sounding from the clouds in the sky and I looked up as I realized that it looked like there was going to be a rainstorm in the city soon.

I lowered my eyes when I realized that another motorcycle was pulling over, this time much closer to me. When I turned my head to see who was doing that, my jaw dropped when I realized it was none other than the guy who dumped me when I most needed him.

Cogwyn, and he looked just like I remembered him, looking at me as if he had something very important to say to me. I froze up where I was, not understanding anymore what was happening. After all these months, when I couldn't even hide my pregnancy by putting on a sweater, he decided to show up?

To say that I was furious would be an understatement and a huge one at that.

Remembering the last words he said to me, I marched up to him. When he got off the bike, I shoved my finger against his chest.

"What are you doing here? Why did you come looking for me?" I stared into his eyes, which was something I stopped doing often. "Did you come here to see how fucked up I am because of you?"

He exhaled, grabbing my hand and moving it away from his chest.

"I didn't come here to mock or make fun of you," he explained, letting go of my hand when he realized I wasn't going to hit him. "I came here because I just learned who ordered the attack against us. Everything finally makes sense."

I took a step away from him, my eyes bulging wide.

"After all this time, after leaving me pregnant, the first thing you say is that you found out about who was behind it?" My eyes checked him out from bottom to top, almost like I was wishing he was nothing more than a ghost. "And the fact I am pregnant – does it mean nothing to you?"

His eyes went down, finally noticing my belly. I was surprised that it took him this long to realize I was pregnant. He was the only and first person I had sex with, so the baby had to be his.

He hurried over to me with semi-open arms. He was trying to show me he was surprised by the fact I was pregnant, that it was huge news to him, but I wasn't going to have any of that.

I put my hand against his chest and shoved him away from me.

"Stay away from me! Stay away from me and my son." I felt a tear coming out and rolling down my cheek. "You've ruined my life. I even considered killing myself because of you."

His facial features softened and he lowered his arms.

"Look, I'm really sorry about everything that happened, but I didn't think that contacting you after we broke up was a good idea, so I decided not to do it." He held my gaze, his eyes filled with something I didn't want to admit was there. "I should've asked you, at least, if you were okay."

I crossed my arms over my chest. "Yeah, you should've done that. There were a lot of things you should've done."

After a moment of silence, he moved his hand so that it was pointing at a bench not too far from us.

"Do you want to sit down with me so that we can talk about it?" When he realized I wasn't going to respond, he added, "And it's really such a nice surprise to know that you're pregnant with my baby. We might not be fated mates, but it's good to know that I'm a father now."

Perhaps it was my Omega instincts that were driving me to go there with him, but either way, we went there. I sat down on it and he was by my side, his hands clasped between his legs.

"I suppose there's nothing I can do to make things better, right?" He asked, looking at my eyes and trying to find out if there was something he could say to make me forgive him.

I shook my head. It was a tough pill for him to swallow, but I knew he could.

"Alright, so let's put behind what I came here for and talk about this," he pointed with both of his hands to my pregnant belly. "You really never thought about calling me to tell me about it this whole time?"

"How was I going to do that when I don't even have your number and you are pretty much someone who doesn't exist on the Internet?"

He nodded, biting his bottom lip. I was right. How was I going to contact someone who was always trying to make himself as invisible as possible from the Internet?

"Then, I just want to say that I'm happy I finally know I'm going to become a father. It's the best news I've had all day."

I examined his eyes, trying to find out if he was telling me the truth or not. It looked like he was, which was a big plus for him. I thought he was just going to look over the fact he put a baby in my belly, but it was the opposite that was happening.

He looked exuberant that he was going to become a dad, even though I had no idea if we would ever live together and if he would have a presence in my baby's life.

I did, however, feel a little closer to him now that he said he was thrilled he was going to become a father.

"And it doesn't matter if you ever forgive me or not – I'm still going to do everything in my power to help the baby and you."

How could my heart fight against someone who was looking so regretful about what he did? Cogwyn wasn't using the exact words I was looking for, but he was still saying he made a mistake when he dumped me and went to do whatever he went to do that time.

His eyes were shimmering with happiness and hope. Cogwyn hoped he could turn my mind around about the fact I didn't like him anymore.

CHAPTER 14

Cogwyn

It was the hugest news all day the fact that Bren was pregnant. I didn't forget about the night we had and I always wondered if he had gotten pregnant, but I didn't contact him to ask if he was feeling better and so, this whole time, I had no idea he was carrying my baby in his belly.

Even though we were never going to find out if the Sphere of Revelations was going to say we were fated mates, everything was happening as if we were.

All I knew was that I couldn't walk away from this. This Omega was pregnant with my baby and I was hoping I could change his mind about what he thought of me. I wanted to bond with him again, to become his Alpha like I was at that time. That time… I was still talking about it like it happened years ago.

I grabbed his hand even though I knew he wasn't going to like it. I thought he was going to pull it back right away, but he didn't do that. He let me caress his hand like we were lovers again.

Tears were rolling down his cheeks and I wished I could dry them with my hands. I needed to do this slowly so that he wasn't spooked.

I was brushing my finger over his hand as I said, "I'm going to do everything for the baby. I'll bust my ass off and buy him everything he needs, and I don't care if he's an Alpha or an Omega, or even a Beta."

The reason why I was saying that was because Betas were looked down upon in our society. People thought that they were outcasts and shouldn't be a part of society.

The reason behind that was pretty simple. Alphas and Omegas formed the perfect pairs and Betas were the middle-ground between us, not being one or the other, and usually preferring hooking up with themselves than with us.

That's one of the reasons why most of the Bear Bikers were Betas and not Alphas. They thought they were inferior to us. They couldn't fit in.

"Ah, fuck it," Bren said all of a sudden, making me wonder what was going on in his mind, but that was only for half of a second. A moment later, he was interlacing his arms around my neck, pulling me to him for a hot kiss.

I couldn't take my lips off of him and I didn't think he wanted me to do that anyway. If anything, he'd always been looking forward to doing this with me and had always wondered what it would be like to kiss me again.

I dug my tongue into his mouth, drilling it in for a short battle. Bren moaned into my mouth and I threw my arms around his body, putting my hand on the back of his head.

As our lips brushed against each other, I couldn't help but feel hard, remembering that time when I penetrated him and everything was better. I was inside of him and I felt like my life was complete. I was wondering if I could do things right this time or if it was hopeless and he was only kissing me now so that he could get his revenge.

After all, Bren had always been a guy who wasn't beyond petty acts of revenge. It would hurt me quite a lot if he was doing this now only to make me think there was some hope for us when, in fact, there wasn't.

He pulled his head back suddenly, regarding me with shimmering eyes.

"Wait, what the hell was that?" I groaned, refusing to move my arms away from him.

"You looked like such a proper daddy for our son that I couldn't resist it."

"Huh?"

"Just shut up and kiss me again," he groaned, pulling me for another hot kiss, my cheeks pressing against his and feeling the wetness of his tears. I never thought I'd ever see someone so snobby being so hungry to kiss me again and again.

I pressed my lips against his lips, moving my hands over his shoulders as I kneaded his skin. I could even feel the beating of his heart and the warmth rising to my cheeks. I could feel my eyes transforming, becoming more like those of a wolf.

I couldn't resist my transformation, knowing that Bren really was the right person for me – the one I had been looking for, this whole time, even though I didn't think that was the case.

Our lips were wet and hot, his breathing quickening. I pulled my head back and settled my hand on his cheek, moving it around and around.

"Uh, wow, that was the best kiss I had in a long time."

"Don't tell me you kissed other guys when I wasn't around."

"No, I didn't," I affirmed, remembering that I had been far too focused on finding out the truth about the attack instead. I had eyes just for him since then, and it made sense that I couldn't find someone who could stir the same kind of fire within me.

I was having difficulty with breathing too, thinking about just one thing right now – taking him to my bed. I couldn't take him to his house. What that Bear Biker asshole told me had to have been right.

It was our Omega fathers who had ordered that hit against us. They thought that us being fated mates would disown their families and bring destruction to their legacies or some bullshit like that.

To be honest, just thinking about it right now was making my stomach churn. Even if it made sense and I had to face my Omega dad about it, I just wanted to pretend I didn't have anything to do with it.

"Good," he purred, pulling me up and taking me to my motorcycle. Why was he doing that? I knew he didn't like Desire.

Well, I supposed it was his love for me that was speaking louder than anything else in his mind that was making him do this right now. "I really think we're made for each other."

"I think the same way," I said, getting back on my bike and putting him in the backseat.

After he wrapped his arms around my torso, he said, "Take me to my home. I want to do this with you there again."

I bit my bottom lip, feeling a little bad that I couldn't grant him his wish.

"There was also something very important I needed to tell you. It's about our Omega fathers..."

I was going to continue my explanation when he covered my mouth with his hand.

"Let's not talk about them right now. I'm okay if you don't want to take me to my home, but please find us a private place where I can feel comfortable with you."

I smiled, tucking those horrible thoughts where they weren't going to be a bother to me.

"That I can do," I purred, riding off on the motorcycle toward my apartment. We crossed through several streets before getting there and I kicked the door open when we arrived.

I was holding him in my arms, wishing we had a better place to do this. My dick was so hard in my pants that it was pushing up against them. I started to pepper his neck with several kisses, loving the feel of his skin against my lips.

"You are my love. I thought I could stop thinking about you after we broke up, but in the end, I was wrong about that as well," I admitted, holding his gaze for what appeared to be an eternity.

"Something about that tells me I knew it was always going to happen," he murmured when I put him down on my bed. A moment later, I climbed up on top of him.

When I lowered my head so that I was devouring his neck with my lips, he started to squirm and say over and over again how much he needed me.

The way he was saying that was making me feel even more turned on than I was before, my shaft hard and leaking my pre-come.

"Say it to me how much you love me," I demanded of him, my hands groping his body and feeling every one of his curves. And they were just perfect, his body begging for me to be inside of him right now.

"I love you more than any other person in the world," he groaned, answering me. The way he said that made me feel like ripping the clothes off of his body, which I did a moment later.

When he was naked and breathing hard, sweat pooling on his forehead and in his armpits, I knew that the moment I had been waiting for since our breakup was finally happening, and I was a much happier man for it.

CHAPTER 15

I didn't think it was going to happen, but when Cogwyn was saying those sweet things to me and how he was promising me he was going to try to be a good father to our son, no matter what I said, I couldn't resist it and so I kissed him.

We connected our lips and since then I couldn't stop thinking about him, even though most of that was because he was right on top of me, grinding his body against me over and over.

I was a little bigger now and heavier, my belly rubbing against his abs, but it was okay. Cogwyn was still the same ruthless guy I knew he was, but he was being more careful with me this time.

He roamed his hands over my body, stopping when they were underneath my asscheeks. He squeezed them, moving down over the bed as he put his tongue out of his mouth and started to lick my junk. I groaned and grabbed his hair, pulling him down further so that he was all over my shaft and balls, his lips so hungry for more.

Meanwhile, I was thinking about the life we were going to have together, not even remembering the fact that he mentioned something about our Omega fathers and how they were involved in something I had no idea about.

"Gosh, this is almost too much," I moaned, putting my hands on his back and digging my fingers into his skin. His body was a little slick thanks to his sweat, which I was loving. The sweat was making our bodies wetter, pre-come coming out through my slit.

"Tell me if you need a moment to catch your breath," he groaned into my ear as he turned me around so that I was on all fours on the bed. My body was shivering. I was worried he was going to penetrate me and fuck me even though I was already pregnant. I didn't want to do anything that could hurt the baby.

He inched closer to me, his body touching mine and engulfing it.

When he neared his mouth to my ear again, I knew that he was going to say something about that.

"Don't worry – I'm going to be kind, just like last time."

And I knew he was going to be, even though it wasn't going to make things any easier for me. As he grabbed my ass and pulled me to him, I felt his dick nudging my entrance. Cogwyn was torturing me by teasing me and even though he knew how evil that was, he was smiling as he showed me how much he was enjoying this.

"I know you're going to," I purred, thrusting my ass against his dick as I felt the need for him to be inside of me right away.

When he was through the first barrier and then was lodged inside of me, I felt like stars were exploding in my mind.

This beast of a man, who was already turning and becoming more like a wolf, was going to knot me and become one with me. He moved his hands around my body as he put them on my belly, caressing it.

"I'm just so happy I'm going to be a father," he said as he started to thrust in and out, his pace slow in the beginning. It was almost too slow and even though I thought that way about it, I was still enjoying it.

I even put my legs over his shoulders so that I was even closer to him than I should be.

When he picked up his pace, I was sad that it meant we were almost done. His balls started to slap against my asscheeks, his body becoming one with mine just like I thought it was going to be.

He locked his eyes with me as his dick grew inside of me, knotting me. Moments later, it was throbbing and erupting inside my tunnel, painting it in white with his come. I closed my eyes and came at the same time, my body rocking and convulsing.

Moments later, I reopened my eyes and all I could see was his face. His eyes were shimmering with happiness and love, and I knew how much it meant to him that we were doing this.

His dick was still so big inside of me.

"Holy shit, that was incredible," I moaned, my hands grabbing his shoulders because I didn't want to feel like I wasn't doing enough. This was incredible. It was the second time I was having sex in my life and it was almost as good as the first time. The only thing I regretted about it was that I wasn't going to get pregnant again.

"I'm ready to do more of this with you when you want to, my love," he murmured into my ear, kissing the side of my neck as he made me squirm against his massive body.

I cracked open a gentle smile as I read his eyes and I knew he was telling the truth.

Seconds later, and I said this as I felt a little sad about it, his dick started to return to its normal shape as I knew we were reaching the end of it.

I wished we could do just one more thing to make tonight more special, almost like it was our wedding night and it was supposed to be a moment that should forever be in our minds.

He pulled out of me when I was parting my lips to say to him what was in my mind.

He brushed his hand over my cheek as he finally realized I had a dirty, little proposition for him.

"Something on your mind?" He asked, his eyes gleaming under the moonlight coming through the windows.

"I want to feel you inside of me again."

He curled up the side of his lips, saying, "But you just did. I knew you were always hungry for me, but I never thought you were so insatiable."

"It's way more than that. There's something I just never did with you."

He widened his eyes slightly as he showed confusion.

He was just opening his mouth when I pushed him against the bed, putting myself right over his dick. It was already semi-hard, but if I worked on it long enough, I was pretty sure I could make it hard again.

"What are you doing-" he groaned as I wrapped my lips around his cockhead and started to suck on it, swirling my tongue under the underside of it, making him throw his head backward.

I took my mouth off of his dick just to say, "Do you like it?" When I smacked my lips, I felt that they were sticky with his pre-come. "I myself am enjoying this very much."

"You're naughtier than I thought you were," he said as he smiled gently. I was all over his dickhead again, swirling my tongue around it and suckling on it. He was so tasty and salty, which was just the way I liked it.

He drew in a short breath as he grabbed my hair and thrust my head down, making me deepthroat him. It came out of nowhere and I was surprised by it, but I wasn't shocked. I wasn't going to say I had any experience deep-throating a man, but I was already getting used to it.

He was so deep inside of my mouth and throat that I couldn't even use my tongue the way I wanted to. Nevertheless, I could feel that he was enjoying this, his breathing quickening as I knew he was close to climaxing again.

"I'm only going to stop this when you're coming inside my mouth," I said after taking my mouth off of his cock.

"I can't wait for that, then," he joked, and I went back to where I was, deep-throating him as much as I could until he was climaxing inside my mouth, his dick shaking and convulsing like it was a trapped beast.

I pulled my head back and kissed his cockhead, loving the way his hands were groping my body as he showed me he still hadn't had enough of me.

I plopped down on the bed as I hugged him and buried my body in his arms. I could even hear his heart beating in his chest, my lips already looking for his lips because I needed one more thing to feel connected to him.

CHAPTER 16

Cogwyn

I woke up and wondered what I was going to get us to eat in the morning. Snowflakes were falling from the sky outside and I could tell that it was already winter – or at least, I was re-membering that it was.

My mind had been so worried about that revelation about the attack that I hadn't even stopped to think about the weather and what my days were like. All I knew was that I was getting stressed out over little things that didn't matter at all.

He was still in my arms, his body snuggled up in mine. I just wanted to hold him in my arms like this for the rest of my life, even though I knew it wasn't possible.

That day outside looked beautiful and I just wanted to go there and play in the snow with him.

I was just turning my head to look back at him when I realized he was opening his eyes again. Seconds later, Bren was looking at me and wondering what I was thinking.

"Is it morning already?" He asked, sounding lazy.

"It is, but you don't need to get off the bed if you don't want to."

And I was still trying to come up with the right way to tell him that we were going to go for takeout because I didn't have any-thing in the kitchen. I didn't have food, utensils, and pretty much everything else I needed to make a proper breakfast for him.

I was caressing his cheek when I said, "It's snowing outside."

"It is?" He asked, sounding lazy as he kept his head on my chest. "I had no idea we were even in the Winter season already. I thought it was Fall."

"I'm just as surprised as you are."

Meanwhile, I was wondering how I was going to approach the subject of his father being one of the culprits who ordered the attack. I know that it was a very delicate subject and I didn't want to ruin this perfect morning we were having.

Minutes passed and we didn't do anything. When I checked the clock on the side table, I realized that it was already ten in the morning and that his stomach was rumbling.

"Hungry? I guess you're going to be disappointed. I can't cook."

That was something about me I tried to hide from him, until now. I'd never cooked in my life. I never had to, after all.

"Really?" He asked, making me feel worried that I was going to lose him again because I was disappointing him. But then, he smiled gently. "I also don't know how to cook, so if we live together we'll certainly have to hire someone to fill that role."

I smiled back at him, sat up on the bed, and then got off of it. I was naked and I noticed that he was checking me out as I started to put my clothes on.

It was like we never broke up and had always been together. Things were developing so quickly since he reappeared in my life that it was kind of scary. But it was scary in a good way, too.

When I was turning around, Bren got off the bed and put on his clothes. I looked at his belly, wondering how many months he had left until the baby was born.

We went outside and I took him to one of his favorite restaurants. No takeout. I was lying when I said we were going to go for takeout. We didn't have much money, especially because his Omega father kept most of their money for himself, but we had enough for breakfast.

We were just walking out of the restaurant when I put my

hand on his shoulder and guided him to one of the alleyways, where we had the privacy we needed to talk about something important.

"The food was delicious," he purred, connecting his lips against my mouth again.

"I'm glad you liked it," I said, feeling sad that our breakfast was already over. I wished that nothing could be changed, living this dream with him for the rest of my life, but the truth was that I couldn't hide from it. "But… I need to go back to what I was going to say to you when I found you."

His body became tense all of a sudden, eyes trembling.

"Can't we just forget it entirely? Can't we just forget the city, our families, and just go and live somewhere else where none of those things can bother us?"

I sighed, realizing just how important that was to him. It would be nice if we could make that happen, but things weren't like in the movies. We needed to face the truth before it crashed against us.

"Unfortunately, my love, we can't," I said.

"I was really afraid of this," he said, lowering his head while I refused to move my hands away from his shoulders. I just wanted to be as close to him as I could be.

I took a deep breath in before I finally said, "Our Omega fathers… They were the ones who ordered the attack. They don't want us together. They thought we could never know that we really are fated mates, just like that foreseer told us."

He snapped his head back up, his eyes locking with mine.

"You're kidding, right? Please tell me you are. It doesn't make any sense."

"Love, I know that it doesn't make sense, but I did some digging and… It's true. You believe me, right?"

He shook his head, stepping away from me even though I had my hands on his shoulders.

"It just can't be possible. This can't be happening. I know

Ranulf and I know that he would never do anything that could harm his husband. They were in love. They always said they'd always do anything for each other."

"I know you are having difficulty believing me about it, but why would I lie? I love my Omega father as well. I'm just as disappointed and angry as you are."

He whirled around, his eyes locking with my eyes again. They studied my expression as he tried to find out what I was thinking. When he realized I really wasn't lying or was hiding part of the truth, he succumbed to his knees.

I went to him right away, putting my arms around him as he started to sob and cry.

"I'm really sorry about it."

He was still crying on my shoulder when he said, "Ranulf tried to kill us. I just can't believe it. I need to confront him and tell the police what we know."

"I don't think we should tell the police about it."

He pulled his head back, looking at me with disbelief in his eyes.

"Why not? They'll be able to confirm your information and do what they need to do. After all, this whole time, they haven't been able to do anything worthwhile for the case."

"I just don't trust them. Not to mention that, when they see it's a biker telling them that, the first thing they'll do is to ignore what I know."

He exhaled and stood up with me. We went back to Desire and I put him on the backseat, feeling his arms wrapping around my torso.

"I understand. So, what do you think we should do?"

"I need to sneak up into my father's room and find out if there's anything there I can use against him. After all, we need solid proof that he did what we know."

And it was going to be somewhat easy to do that. He still had no idea that I knew what I knew. It was just going to be a little more difficult to get into the house. After all, I hadn't gone there in a very long time - ever since they kicked me out because I wanted to become a biker.

"I'm going to find out everything I can in my father's office and his room."

I snapped my head to look over my shoulder and find his trembling eyes. "No, you don't need to do that. Leave it to me. I don't want you risking yourself and our little one."

He cracked open a smile, shaking his head. "Don't worry. I'm not going to do anything I haven't already done. After all, how many times do you think I entered his room when he locked it from me?"

I knew he felt confident about it, but I still couldn't help but worry about him.

CHAPTER 17

Opening the door, I still found myself in Ranulf's room. I looked behind my shoulder and I didn't see him or hear him coming anywhere near here. The house was quite silent in this cold and snowy morning, snowflakes falling outside.

Alright, I was here in his room and I could see he had left many memories of his marriage to my Alpha father. Their portraits together, pictures, trophies, mementos, and that sort of stuff dotted the room, and it all made me think that Cogwyn's information had to be wrong.

Perhaps it was more like a suspicion than the truth… I was kind of hoping it was so that we could focus on the most important thing at hand and find the true culprits. That would be much easier than knowing it was my father's husband the one who ordered his death.

Or perhaps something happened in the attack that he couldn't quite tell me about? Maybe something went wrong? I didn't know, but I was curious.

I peeked over my shoulder when I thought I heard a pair of footsteps approaching the door. Ranulf didn't know this about me, but I was quite good at sneaking around and opening doors. He was probably still thinking that I was in my room, brooding about the fact I was pregnant and didn't know what was happening to

Cogwyn.

The door to the room was closed. I'd hear him opening it before he had the chance to find out that I was here. I wasn't going to leave his things where they weren't before. I was going to be meticulous in my search.

Hopefully, this wasn't going to take too long, either.

I went to his desk, opened the top drawer, and I wasn't surprised when I found only paper sheets after paper sheets detailing his business decisions. He worked home office for a multinational company, in their PR department, and thus there wasn't anything worthwhile here.

I'd once considered working a similar job as him, but then I realized it wasn't for me. I didn't look it, but I was thinking about becoming a PE teacher. So many of my high school teachers said I had the natural attributes to become one.

Opening another drawer, I wasn't surprised when I still didn't find what I came here for. I mean, did I think I really was going to find the information I needed in his office?

The police had already finished a thorough search of the place and didn't find anything. They didn't think he was one of the perpetrators, but they still needed to do that because it was part of their operation.

I pressed my hand against my back, feeling the weight of the belly. I moved my hand over it in small circles as I thought more and more about the life I was thinking about having with my... husband.

I chuckled. Thinking that way about Cogwyn was something I'd thought would never happen, but here I was, thinking that nothing else could feel righter than that.

I opened a couple more drawers, looked behind the books in his bookshelves, under the bed, and pretty much everywhere else I could think of, only to realize I was probably out of luck.

I stood up and was turning around when I realized that the door was already open and in front of it was standing the man who I had even stopped thinking about. It wasn't that I forgot about him, but that I didn't think he was going to show up so soon – and especially without my knowing about it.

I froze up. It was too late. Ranulf knew that I was in his room without his knowledge and okay, and he looked pretty disappointed that I went behind his back.

He clasped his hands behind his back, coming toward me. His footsteps were composed and controlled, almost like he was doing everything in his power not to lash out at me right now.

"I was looking for something."

A moment of silence when he stopped walking, standing a couple of feet across from me. "Are you going to tell me why, or do I have to take that information out of you?"

"Cogwyn said you were the one who ordered the attack against us. You killed your own husband."

He widened his eyes. "I'm surprised that you are back together again. Or maybe I shouldn't be. Someone told me that he saw you with him in a rundown apartment building in the middle of nowhere. You disappointed me more by doing that than sneaking into my room and looking through my stuff."

"He also said that you ordered the attack because you didn't like that we are fated mates, just like that foreseer said we are. The Sphere of Revelations…"

"Yes, it was going to confirm it and I couldn't have it."

I widened my eyes, finding it unbelievable that he was confirming everything to me without giving it a second thought. His expression was so serene I couldn't even try reading what he was thinking right now.

"You're being far too calm about this. Are you thinking about killing me here as well? I looked up to you when I was growing up."

"And you stopped being like that when you met Cogwyn for the first time. He started to change you. You became more rebellious because of him, fighting me and Parth because you had such a huge crush on him you couldn't control yourself…"

"The fact I had a crush on him didn't change anything about me."

"How not?" He asked, curling up the corner of his lips. He lifted his right hand as he pointed it to me and said, "You've gotten pregnant and I know that he's the father. He's the only person you ever had sex with."

I blushed. "I didn't think you were keeping tabs on that. I thought that my personal life was just that."

"It is and I care about you – more so than you think I do. There's a good reason why I didn't want you two together."

I didn't say anything for the next minute or so, holding his gaze for as long as I could.

"So, you're really confirming that you were behind the attack. You betrayed the Wolf Shifters by asking those Bear Bikers to come after us."

A tear broke out and rolled down his cheek.

"You know, I really loved your father. Parth was everything to me, but then cracks started to show up in our married life, and we didn't know how to deal with them. He was even thinking about sleeping in a separate room. Of course, it didn't end up happening because he didn't have enough time, but he said he was thinking about it."

"I hope that wasn't enough reason for you to kill him. He didn't deserve it."

"I wasn't the one who came up with the plan."

I widened my eyes, surprised more than anything that he was finally confirming what I came here for. It turned out that I wasn't going to need solid proof to confront him about it.

I was already recording this conversation and I was going to give it to the police so that they could lock him up.

"I'm disappointed in you. I actually came here looking for proof that you didn't do what Cogwyn accused you of."

"No, he's partially right. It was Eleric the one who came with the crazy plan to attack you when you were in the church. I tried to convince him to change his mind, but it was too late. He was already hell-bent on getting rid of both of you.

I did say that he shouldn't kill our husbands, that only Cogwyn had to die, but of course, the Bear Bikers fucked it up."

I took a step backward. He just said that they were only supposed to kill my lover and spare everyone else. I thought that they were supposed to kill all of us.

He took a step toward me when his eyes went down and he realized that my phone was in the pocket of my pants.

He leaped toward me, trying to grab it out of my pocket, but then I turned around quickly and started to race out of the house. I needed to get to Cogwyn as fast as possible and before Ranulf had enough time to order his bodyguards to grab me.

I needed to transfer the recording to Cogwyn's phone. When he had it and also the evidence he was looking for in his former house, he would then have enough to put our Omega fathers behind bars.

I was just going out of the property when I felt his hand grabbing my shoulder, and then he yanked me to him with enough force to make me fall over on my ass.

When I looked up, I realized that I had fucked things beyond repair.

CHAPTER 18

Cogwyn

"**I** can't believe you did what you did," I said, growling as I felt my canines growing. I was growing bigger, my body beginning to press against my clothes. I didn't want to turn and become a wolf in front of my Omega father, but the way he was looking at me with such disdain on his face was infuriating.

I thought that I was going to come here and find out I was wrong about it, but when he realized that I was coming back home after years of being away from it, he decided to reveal everything and speak to me like he knew he would never be locked up for his crime.

"If you came here really looking for information that I wasn't involved in the attack, then you were a fool. I was one of the few who knew about what was going to happen in the church. I didn't want my family's pride to be tarnished by you getting married to that Omega. He didn't deserve you. He deserved someone much better."

I fisted my hand, doing everything in my power not to punch him in his face so hard that teeth would pop out of his mouth. After all, he was still my father and I still respected him a lot, even though a lot of that respect was gone now.

"You killed your own husband. He was a good person."

A tear broke out and rolled down his cheek.

"Yes, he was, but I didn't want my family to be linked to his family because of you. I didn't even want to remember that you existed." He glanced me over with disdain, wishing he could get rid of me right at this moment.

"Perhaps you should hate me more. I'm going to lock you up in prison myself."

He burst out laughing, regaining his composure moments later. "Based on what? Your word against mine? Do you think the police will trust a biker? If anything, they'll make use of the opportunity to lock you up instead."

I curled up the sides of my lips. I fished my phone out of my pocket and showed it to him.

"Perhaps you should know that I've been recording our conversation this whole time. This should be more than enough to convince the police."

His eyes darted down, lips trembling.

"You fucking asshole," he growled, leaping toward me, but I punched him in his face and stomped on him. I pinned him against the floor, locking my eyes with his.

"You can't stop this anymore. I'm going to have my justice." I pressed my foot more strongly against his chest. I was doing everything in my power not to kill him right now, even though he deserved it. "You should be feeling thankful that Bren convinced me not to kill you."

"Maybe you should do that," he growled when his bodyguards stormed into the room, pointing their guns at me. They were packing silver bullets and they knew that one shot would be enough to immobilize me. More than one shot hitting me and I'd be dead.

The window was open and I jumped through it, landing outside as I raced over to my motorcycle. I plopped down on the seat and fired up the engine, the tires screeching as I raced over to Bren. We chose a meet-up spot so that we could discuss our findings.

I peeked over my shoulders and I couldn't see the bodyguards chasing me, which was concerning. Unless they were planning something I couldn't even begin to guess what it was, they had to be coming after me. I had the recording of my father's confession. I knew that it was going to be enough to put him behind bars.

I pulled over and jumped off the bike as I went into the alleyway. I thought I was going to find Bren in there and already waiting for me, but he was nowhere to be seen. I looked left and right, my heart pounding in my chest.

When I thought I was beginning to hear the rumbling of motorcycles' engines in the distance, my phone started to buzz in the pocket of my pants.

Brent was the only one who had my phone number and I knew that it had to be him. It couldn't be anyone else. Remembering that he was pregnant, I couldn't help but worry about his wellbeing. He needed to pull through and come out of this alive and better than before.

I fished my phone out of my pocket before examining the screen. My hand was trembling when I realized that it was a phone call but that I hadn't picked it up in time.

Shit. Did that mean he tried to call me other times before? I would never forgive myself if he ended up getting hurt because of me. After all, he was only involved in this because of me. I shouldn't have told him about what I knew.

No time to waste, I thought. The Bear Bikers were already coming where I was and I was pretty sure that, this time, they were going to shoot me until they made sure I was dead. They weren't going to make the same mistake twice.

I jumped back on my bike, started the engine, and then rode away to Bren's house. As the wind blew against my face, I had no idea if I was going to have enough time to save him.

All I knew was that I was already getting the police involved in this. Even though I knew that meant probably getting myself locked up too, at least I was going to make sure he was going to be safe.

After all, I had no idea how his Omega father was going to react to him knowing that his son knew about his involvement in the attack.

The tires screeched to a halt as I pulled over, realizing that Ranulf had Bren pinned against the ground in front of his house. He was on top of him, his face showing how much he hated his son.

His bodyguards had me surrounded at a moment's notice, pointing their guns at me. I lifted my hands over my head as I didn't want to do anything that could piss him off.

"Ranulf, I have no idea what he told you, but I already gave the police everything I know, including the recording Bren made of you. They already know about this and they're coming here. Whether you like it or not, you are going to jail, and you'll have a lot to explain about this."

He scoffed, keeping his food pressed against my lover's back.

"The police won't do anything."

After a moment of silence as I realized we weren't going to be making much progress, I said, "I didn't know you hated your son so much. I thought that he meant a lot more to you."

A tear broke out and rolled down his cheek. "I love my son, but I don't want him to end up with you. He deserves someone much better. Everything got so much worse when we realized he was pregnant with your baby."

"I'll do everything in my power to make sure my love is safe."

The skin under his left eye twitched, showing me that he really didn't like that I loved Bren.

He pulled a gun out of his pants, pointing it at me. I felt my eyes changing, becoming more like a wolf's. My canines became bigger as I felt the other side of me coming out.

"I'm not going to let you take my son away from me. I know the kind of person you are. You will destroy the sweet person he is."

"I would never do anything that could hurt him," I promised, hearing the sound of a bullet coming out of his gun and perforating my chest, my body falling backward over the floor as I realized what was happening.

Ranulf shot me with a silver bullet, and I was going to die.

"Cogwyn!" Bren yelled, leaping toward me. He was right by my side, his hands pushing and nudging me as he tried to make me look at him.

He put his hand on the side of my face, turning my head so that I could look at him. One last look at the face of the man who meant so much to me. The pain in my chest was terrible and was making me think that the bullet most likely hit one of my vital organs. If that was the case, then chances were I wasn't going to pull through.

"You're going to be okay. I promise," Bren murmured when I lost consciousness and didn't know if I was going to wake up again.

BREN'S EPILOGUE

Alright, there was this one thing Cogwyn loved that I just had to bring to him. I opened the door to his room, finding it a little sad that he was still in the hospital bed and that it didn't look like he was going to wake up anytime soon. At least he didn't die… yet, but the police had already said that, if he came out of the coma, they'd lock him up.

I couldn't let that happen. I wasn't going to.

I wasn't worried about that right now, either way. My mind was focused on something else. My ex, Ish, told me that there were a couple of things I could do to remediate the situation. Something that would make Cogwyn remember me and that there were still a couple of things he needed to do, even though he was sleeping.

Sleeping… That's how I liked to think about it. That he was sleeping and that, soon, he'd wake up and realize that I was here, by his side, waiting for him.

My hand was holding a memento from his family. It was a small statue, of a man seated on his motorcycle, doing a wheelie. That was just like him. I remembered that this was in both of his rooms where I had been with him and I was pretty sure that it meant a lot to him.

Outside, I could see the sun shining through the clouds. Winter was ending and I was already looking forward to the coming season.

I pulled a chair, sitting down on it as I opened a book. I was going to read a story to Cogwyn. One other thing Ish said, which I really was happy about, was that me speaking could trigger Cogwyn's brain to wake him up.

Something needed to be done, and I wasn't going to spend my days hoping that he was going to get out of his coma without my help. I was stubborn like that.

I read the first pages of the book after putting down, on the side table, the small statue that I'd found in his belongings. Outside of the room was a police officer. He was just one of the many that were always here in case Cogwyn regained his consciousness.

I didn't pay much attention to him, focusing on the story that I was reading. I thought that my eyes picked up a twitch of his finger, but that couldn't be true. I even stopped reading the words to look up and check his hand, but it was immobile like before and it looked like it was in the same position, too.

I continued reading the story out loud as I noticed, this time, his hand moving and going to his chest. I froze up. This couldn't be happening, right? Cogwyn couldn't be waking up after months of being in a coma.

I was still pregnant and my belly was so much bigger now. If there was a moment for him to wake up, then it was now. Not much longer from now and I'd be delivering the baby…

I dropped the book when I realized that his eyelids were moving up and down, his eyes looking at the ceiling.

"Oh, gosh. My head hurts so much," he mumbled, his hand palming his chest as he pulled one of the cords that were around his body. "What the hell is this?"

I jumped off the chair right away, putting myself right in front of his eyes so that he could see me.

"Bren?" He asked, his voice low and weak. "I knew I could smell you."

"I can't believe you are finally awake!" I exclaimed, smiling from ear to ear.

"That… I'm finally awake?" He asked, narrowing his eyes slightly. "What do you mean? What happened?"

I stepped away from him, not sure how I should approach the subject with him. I didn't want to make him feel more concerned about what happened than he was.

He sat up on the bed, the heart monitoring machine beeping more loudly.

"Tell me everything that happened, Bren. I deserve to know."

"You went into a coma. You've been in a coma here for months since then. I've been waiting this whole time for you to wake up."

He widened his eyes, blinking twice. He looked at his hands as he said, "I'm sorry."

"You don't have anything to be sorry about. It wasn't your fault that things happened this way." Putting my arms out wide, I exclaimed, "But it's really so good to see that you're feeling better. It's like a dream come true."

His eyes darted down, noticing my belly. "I can see that you aren't lying about this, not that I thought you were going to lie about it anyway. Your belly is so much bigger now. I'm going to become a father soon. I suppose I got lucky again."

"You did," I said. "The doctors said that if the bullet had hit you a couple of inches to the right, you'd be dead now."

He curled the side of his lips, chuckling. "I've always been lucky. It's one of the reasons why I ended up falling in love with someone so incredible."

I felt a tear breaking out and rolling down my cheek. "I'm just so fucking happy that you're back."

I ran over to him, hugging him tightly as I buried my head in the crook of his neck. I was sobbing as he put his hand behind my head, drawing small circles on it.

"Shh, don't worry. I'm really back and I'm not going anywhere this time. Once the doctors give me the go-ahead, I'll get out of here and we'll leave the city. I don't think there's any more space for us here."

I was still sobbing when I pulled my head back, looking at his eyes. "Everything will be so much better, but there's something you should know before then."

"What thing?" He asked, lifting his right eyebrow. "You should tell me everything before I get out of this bed."

"It's that the police want to lock you up when you're feeling better," I stammered, wishing that things weren't like this.

He looked over my shoulder, realizing that there was a police officer in front of the door. He had his back turned to us and the wall was thick enough to make it so our conversation wasn't leaking.

Cogwyn pushed the white bedsheet off of his body, groaning as he realized he still felt a lot of pain.

I supported him using the weight of my body, letting him put his arm over my shoulders.

"Be careful. You're a shifter, but you're still human like I am. We need to get out of here before he realizes you're awake."

He regained his balance, now looking like he could stand on his feet without my help. I looked from left to right, wondering what he was scheming.

"What are you planning?" I asked.

"You should draw him into the room and I'll knock him out when he isn't looking."

The plan was very simple, but it should be effective. I went to the door, opened it, and then pointed to the bed as I said hurriedly, "He escaped! I don't know what happened, but when I came into the room, he wasn't in his bed anymore."

"How the hell did he get out?" The police officer asked, drawing out his gun as he started to search the room.

Cogwyn punched the side of his head with his elbow, and the officer's eyes went into his head as he lost consciousness. He fell over on the floor, his gun falling out of his hand.

Cogwyn picked it up and went with me to the hallway. Out in the distance, where the hallways connected, we could see some hospital staff members walking from one room to the other.

"All right, how are we going to do this?" I asked, standing slightly behind him because he was the one who was going to take the lead.

"Just follow me. It's not the first time I've been to this hospital."

I widened my eyes slightly, wondering what story there was in what he said. I didn't have enough time to ask him about that, so I followed him out of the hospital. We had some close calls, but in the end, we soon were in the parking lot.

Cogwyn groaned, looking left and right as he said, "I knew that my bike wasn't here."

COGWYN'S EPILOGUE

Desire wasn't in the hospital's parking lot, but I managed to find it at the police station. It took me some trying and I had to figure out some things about the way things worked there, but I still managed to get my motorcycle back.

We were now living somewhere else, a small house in the woods, where I could hunt, could be happy with my lover, and I could start anew. We were even making new friends, and one of them was an Omega like my lover was.

He was with Bren, holding our baby in his arms. He had such a big and bright smile on his face. I wondered if he was thinking the same thing, that he should also build a family after finding the right person for him.

On my shoulder was a rabbit that I caught when I was hunting in the woods, my feet crunching the snow. Nefion was such a good person I couldn't help but wonder why he was still single and never found someone he wanted to hook up with.

He snapped his head up when he realized I was coming. Cogwyn was just coming out of the house, his hand holding a casserole as he realized that I was already coming back from my hunt.

"Oh, Cogwyn. I didn't realize you were already back. I was just playing with your kid and showing him some new tricks I can do with my hands." And as he finished saying that, he did said tricks, earning some laughs from my baby.

"Well, I'm happy that you two are getting along," I said after putting my rifle down and wrapping my arm over my lover's shoulders. I kissed the side of his face and then his lips, making sure that the kiss wasn't going to last long because I didn't want to make Nefion feel uncomfortable.

I picked up the baby from his arms, loving the fact that he was already moving his small hands toward me, showing me that he recognized I was his father. I rubbed my snot against his face, saying a couple of things over and over that didn't make any sense to me, but which made him chuckle.

The sound of his chuckles was like music to my ears.

Bren handed him the casserole with delicious, homemade food in it, and Nefion picked it up. He lifted the cover and took a peek at it, saying, "Thanks. I'm really going to enjoy this food."

"Please, come back for more. We're trying to fit in."

"I know, it's just that I've got a party that I'm going to throw at my place tonight. I don't suppose you want to come, right?"

"No, we can't," Bren explained, grabbing my hand. "We still haven't managed to find a babysitter for our little one."

"Oh, I could be his babysitter. After all, we get along so well and I always make him laugh."

I looked at Bren, who smiled. "Sure, why not? Wanna start tomorrow?" I asked, remembering that Bren was looking into getting a job and I wanted to be out hunting more often. It looked like the perfect fit, didn't it? Nefion taking care of our little one, Bren fitting in, and me hunting and becoming more like a man of the woods.

Even Desire was beginning to collect some dust in the garage. Don't get me wrong – I still loved riding on my motorcycle, but out here, so far from civilization and hiding from the police in another state, I didn't have another option.

"Then, it's settled. I'll start tomorrow. Should I come here in the morning?"

"Sure, and then maybe you could even start living here with us. Don't worry. We don't have a lot of money, but we'll still pay you fairly for your job. You deserve it."

"Thanks," he said, turning around with the casserole in his hands. "I'm going now, but I'm excited for tomorrow already."

And having said that, he put the casserole on the seat of his car, turned on the engine, and then drove off. We watched until we couldn't see him anymore behind the trees.

We went into the house and I put the baby in his crib, closing the door of his room after cranking up the heater.

I turned, looking at my husband as I lifted his hand and admired the ring on his finger. We got married here, right on this mountain. It was perfect and the snow was always present here. It was always also a little cold, but it wasn't anything that we couldn't handle and we both loved the colder temperatures anyway.

I put my hand on the back of his head, pulling it up for a kiss.

Our lips connected, his body melting in my arms as I had to hold him with my other arm so that he didn't fall.

I pulled my head back, gazing into his eyes as I said, "I love you so much. There's nothing I can do that can express that enough."

"You're wrong. There's one thing," he said, his hand groping my ass and taking off my belt.

"Really? And what would that be?" I asked, feeling my pants dropping as he snuck his fingers under my briefs and looped them around my shaft.

"Making love with me," he answered when I pushed him toward the bed, his body plopping down on it as I climbed on top of him, ripping the clothes off of his body as I started to wet his entrance. Making another baby with my Omega? Sign me up, I thought.

It would be perfect.

The End

The next page has a sneak peek of the first book of this series.

Go check it out! And leave a review if you liked the book. It always helps me so much!

SNEAK PEEK: OMEGA FOR OBSESSIVE ALPHA

Wolf Shifter MPREG Fated Mates Romance (Omegaverse MC - 1)

Feran

I felt something sniffing me, like he was trying to smell me. I cracked open my eyes as I found someone standing right in front of me. It was a man, huge, older than me, and hot as balls. The moment my eyes set on him, it was like fireworks exploded in my head.

I wanted to rip his clothes off his body and see what he was like naked. I wanted to slide my tongue over his muscles, to feel him for the man he was, to grind my body against his, and to make sweet love with him. I was already drooling even though I didn't even notice that yet.

The guy who was in front of me was so close I could smell the minty odor coming out of his mouth. His eyes were emerald green, his hair messy and blond, some stubble on his chin. His face was chiseled and followed hard lines, making me want to put my hand on it and feel it until he was smiling.

And I just noticed I was supposed to be falling to the floor.

I felt something holding me in place so that that didn't happen. It was his arm, wrapped around my torso. It was firm, showing off his confidence. I was still in the same room from before, which was behind the bar where I was drinking away my sorrows.

I just remembered something terrible that happened not too long ago, which made me come running to this place. I supposed I should be thankful he was holding me like this so that I didn't fall and hurt myself, but the way he was smelling me was also frightening and annoying. I should be shoving him away from me as fast as possible and as hard as I could, but that was easier said than done.

I wasn't going to say that I was skinny. In fact, I was lean and I did work out, but I didn't follow any diet and I didn't inject my body with anything. This guy, on the other hand, looked more like a gym rat than anything.

And he was even more frightening because his body was covered in tattoos. There was even one of them, which caught my attention the most, sneaking from under his shirt and going across his neck. It was the tattoo of a lone wolf, making me remember that he was probably from *that* MC gang. I shivered at the thought of having caught the attention of one of them. It was the worst thing that could be happening.

Not to mention that I didn't have anything to do with him...

He parted his lips, blowing a bigger cloud of his mouth's odor over my face. I closed my eyes and scrunched up my nose, but not because I was turned off by the smell, but because his scent was overwhelming.

As an Omega, I was always subjected to this kind of situation, especially when the other guy was an Alpha. And it wasn't just the smell coming out of his mouth that was making me hard and aroused right now. It was also his musky scent, which came from all around his body.

"I just saved you from hurting yourself. I think you should be thanking me." And as soon as he finished saying that, he smiled, showing me his perfect teeth. I always thought that bikers like him didn't brush their teeth, but it looked like he was an exception.

I knew he was a biker because of the patch he had on the front of his leather jacket. It showed that he, indeed, was from one of the biker gangs in the region. They were called the Wolf Bikers, and everyone around here in the city feared them. They were a menace, robbing people and their houses, causing the police all sorts of troubles.

I knew that coming to this bar was a mistake, but I didn't think I was going to run into a member of the Wolf Bikers.

I shot my hands to his chest, shoving them against it. I thought he was going to leave me alone and add some distance between us, but he held his ground, tightening how hard his arm was pressing against my torso...

Yel

I stomped hard onto the grass, my fangs growing bigger. Fisting my hand, I couldn't help but feel like punching that bear biker until blood was gushing out of his mouth. I was going to bash his head against the pavement until his skull cracked, I swore.

I couldn't believe I was so amateur about it. I should have realized someone was going to come after him, too. I was going to make bank by kidnapping Feran.

Stomping on the grass again, all I could do was turn back and stride over to Delight, my bike. It was parked in front of the bar. The members of the Wolf Bikers didn't know that I was here. They didn't frequent this part of town. I was the only one here, and the only one who should have known about Feran.

He was from one of the most important families in the city. I knew that kidnapping him would make me a lot of money. I didn't even feel bad about it, and I wouldn't either way. The money his family would have to hand over wouldn't even dent their fortune, after all.

I couldn't lose this opportunity.

The moon high above the buildings and the houses, I looked up at it as I realized how easy it would have been to turn into a wolf while that Bear Biker was pointing his gun in my direction. In a fair fight, did he think he would win?

Fuck that guy. He'd always been a nuisance. He was keeping tabs on me.

Ennith...

I was going to punch his gut so hard one day he would puke whatever was in his stomach, I swore, swinging my leg over Delight and remembering all the things that happened between us. All the clashes we had, even when he was in school and trying to prove to the teachers he was better than me at pretty much anything. He joined up with the Bears because they were the right fit for him.

Turning on the engine of the motorcycle and propelling it forward, crossing one red traffic light after the other without even putting on my helmet, I was focused on just one thing – finding Ennith and Feran. I was pretty sure I knew where he was taking him to.

The Bear Bikers' hideout.

It wasn't too far and even though I wasn't going to have the support of the Wolf Bikers, I should be okay. I didn't need them, anyway. I was pretty confident in how well I could sneak in and out of that place. It was pretty big, with ample free space. I was going to have to keep my guard up all the time, but it wasn't a challenge impossible to tame.

I smirked, feeling overconfident. I had my gun with me now.

I'd left it in the motorcycle because I didn't think I was going to have to use it during the kidnapping. I thought it was going to be simple. Feran was pretty small, a little lean, weak, and very submissive. Me being the Alpha I was, he was always going to smell me and fall to his knees when his nose got a sniff of it. I mean, everything was going according to plan before Ennith popped up.

I couldn't help but feel aroused by Feran, though. He had short, dark hair, perfect lips, ocean-blue eyes, and lips that were just the right size. When I enclosed my arm around his torso, the first thought that popped up in my mind was how much I wanted to rip the clothes off his body and bend him over. It only didn't happen because raping was something I would never do.

He was about 10 years younger than me, too. That was a piece of information I dug out on the internet. And that age gap was a plus for me, too. If we had met under different circumstances, I'd be going for him for sure. The only problem with that was that now he thought of me just as an asshole who was trying to kidnap him.

Being the person I was, I couldn't care less about that.

I pulled up not too far from their hideout, pushing my motorcycle until it was hidden in a dark and forgotten alleyway between two massive buildings. I pulled up my hood, shadowing my face, and went to one of the doors that two guards were by the side of.

Their hands went to their pistols as soon as they realized someone was padding over to them...

MPREG SERIES AND MORE

SERIES - PREGNANT FOR HIM

1. Controlled by the Alpha 1: An MPREG Omegaverse Story
2. Controlled by the Alpha 2: An MPREG Omegaverse Story
3. Controlled by the Alpha 3: Dominating the Fertile Omega
4. Controlled by the Alpha 4: An Omega's Tale of Obedience
5. Controlled by the Alpha 5: A Tale of Obedient Submission
6. Controlled by the Alpha 6: Monopolized in Outer Space

SERIES - LOST INNOCENCE

1. Overwhelming the Omega 1: His Little Doll
2. Overwhelming the Omega 2: Brute Entry and Double Teamed
3. Overwhelming the Omega 3: His Tight Backdoor
4. Overwhelming the Omega 4: Stretching his Front Door
5. Overwhelming the Omega 5: Until he Spasms
6. Overwhelming the Omega 6: Naïve and Untouched

Straight to gay first time bundles:

1. Stuffed by Blue Collars: The Full Straight to Gay Age Gap Story

2. Throbbing Hard: A Straight to Gay MMF Bundle

3. Teasing Older Men: 16 Straight to Gay MM Stories

4. Helping Hand: 13 Forbidden Older Man Stories

5. So BIG It Hurts MEGA Bundle: 14 Stories of Man of the House, Brats and Gay Sitters

ABOUT THE AUTHOR

Michael Levi's biggest passion? Writing steamy, romantic stories that leave his readers panting. He's currently focusing on ABDL MM romances, but his collection is diverse and there are books for everyone's tastes. If you're looking for straight to gay, first time, BBC, sissification, and more, you're going to find them on his author page.

He lives to pamper his readers, every kiss means a lot more than what meets the eye, and he loves his Alpha males. Making sure that every gay first time feels different, Michael Levi writes his stories with a cup of coffee by his side. And for inspiration, he always opens a photo of his new crush.